LUST AFTER BATTLE

Soldier Girls
and Swordmaidens

The characters and events portrayed in this book are fictitious. Any similarity to real persons, living or dead, is coincidental and not intended by the author. All characters are 18+. These fictions are bedroom fantasies for the imagination, written by adults for the pleasure and enjoyment of adults.

The author grants permission for royalty-free use of these scripts in audio recordings and performances. All other rights reserved.

Copyright © 2023 by redditor u/RavishaGirl.

Cover art by redditor u/RavishaGirl

Scripts originally posted at www.reddit.com/r/gonewildaudio and www.reddit.com/r/ravishagirl

1 To Ravish the Queen of Elves   1

2 Dancing the Blades: Ronin After the Battle   21

3 My Beautiful Warrior   39

4 Succubus Resistance Training, the Night Before
   Battle on the Plains of Hell   52

5 A Sultry Elfgirl Paladin Teaches You How to Kiss
   Her, Titfuck Her, and Cum in Her Mouth   74

6 The Gunslinger Captured: Promise to Let Me Go,
   Bounty Hunter, And You Can Ravish Me   97

7 Tipsy Elf Maid in a Tavern   122

8 This Wounded Elf Priestess Needs You to Heal
   Her With Your Cock   143

9 Queen of the Red Seas   163

10 Elf Girls   173

Look at her, sexy reader. She has won her battle. Drops of blood rained from her blade; smoke rose from her gun. Now her hair is stuck to her cheek with sweat, and her breasts lift and fall beneath her half-unzipped jumpsuit or her barely-there armor as she catches her breath. Her heart is racing. She is flushed and hot. Exhilarated at being alive, she might kiss you. She might duel you. She might mount you and ride you like a stallion into battle. In these pages, you will meet her. She might be an intergalactic gunfighter, or a gunslinger in an old West saloon. She might be the personal bodyguard of an elven queen, or a sultry elfgirl paladin escorting the son of a human chieftain through treacherous woods on his way to an arranged marriage. She might be a war priestess or a pirate captain or a samurai dropping from the trees with her katana. No one has ever fought like she has fought. No one will ever delight you in bed as she will, because there is battle fury in her blood and wild passion in her heart. Come meet her. She's just inside this book. Don't keep her waiting.

Besides the sexy readers, this volume is for all the lovely voices who have performed these tales as erotic audio dramas at /r/gonewildaudio on reddit. The author grants permission for royalty-free use of these scripts in audio recordings and performances. Please credit the author when performing.

1

To Ravish the Queen of Elves

TAGS: [F4M] [Fsub] [Switchy] [Elven Swordswoman] [If It's the Elven Queen's Bed You Seek, You Must First Best Me in Battle, Human Male] [Seduction] [Swordplay] [Tsundere] [Fucked on a Windowsill] [Passion] [Enemies to Lovers] [NonCon] because [Forced Creampie] [Not Pulling Out]

The elfgirl's name is Nikaia, pronounced nee – keye (rhymes with "sky") – ah.

We hear torches guttering. Perhaps exotic music through a window. Then, suddenly, the unsheathing of a blade.

amused Stop right there, human male. Did you really think it was going to be that easy, sneaking into the elf queen's bedchamber by night, with that hard sword clutched in your hand? *teasing laughter*

How DID you get so far into our domain, human? A barechested, sweaty human, in the hall outside the queen's room in the palace, in the heart of the most ancient city of the elves! You can see the elven stars burn in the sky through that narrow window. You can hear the music of conch shell horns, and the night drums of our festival, where elfgirls dance naked beneath the willows and elven men vie for their attention. *haughtily* I suppose your human chieftains thought our holiest festival the best time to send their assassins.

And here you are. I don't know how you got here, barbarian, but you'll go no further. No one molests the queen of elves in her sleep unless he can first best me in battle. And I don't think that's likely. Do you?

Here, I'll step from the shadows into the torchlight to give you a better look. You'll be bleeding in this hall in a few minutes, bold mortal. I'm the last woman you'll ever see. Take a good look.

sultry I am Nikaia. I wield a slender blade in either hand. Their steel shimmers in the torchlight. The steel of my eyes shimmers too, hot as a night on fire. My battle tattoos wind about my arms like flame.

Yes, you're quite taller than me, human male; I'm an elfgirl. *amused* You can tell by my ears. They're curved and pointed. *giggles* Like my blades. And I don't walk like your human girls, do I? My shoulders back, my elven breasts lifted, my breathing deep and full. You like the sight of me, don't you? In my tight leather armor. I am graceful, confident, supple and strong as an ancient tree.

merry laughter at something he says ... Stand aside and you'll be merciful to me??? Arrogant male. The elven queen and I have known each other since we were little girls. I'm not about to let you have her. If you think your height and those

... absurdly thick human muscles ... mmmm ... if you think your biceps give you any advantage over ME, you should know that I've been dancing the blades centuries before you were born.

fierce but amused Guard yourself, human.

clash of blades

her merry laughter Oh, you dance well! And you're so fast.

clash

And strong. Oh, this will be a challenge. I haven't had a real challenge in so long. The human kingdoms should send rugged, masculine assassins after our queen more often.

clash

It's only a matter of time, human. You should give up. You have one sword, I have two. *giggling*

clash

Oh, how your eyes burn as you watch me dance.

clash

As you watch me MOVE. You've never seen a body like this, have you?

clash

breathless A lithe voluptuous, elven body. Graceful as the morning and sleek as the night. Oh, you would like to touch me, wouldn't you, warrior? I see it in your eyes. How you blaze with desire for me. Does it light fire in your loins, dancing the blades with me? *teasing* You won't conquer me, mortal. I can't BE conquered. For all I know, you may be the best swordsman in the human kingdoms, but I am the finest swordswoman of the elves. You will not best me, human barbarian.

clanging of blades

improv her laughter and swordplay

she gasps Oh! That thrust slipped past my guard and cut the leather straps at my shoulder! Mmm, barely grazing my skin. You could have cut off half my head, but instead … you've chosen to cut away half my top. Mmm, see? *breathless* The leather has slipped down and the swell of my left breast is soffft … and naked. Just a few battle sigils inked into my skin.

The night air through that window feels good on my breast. I should thank you, warrior.

clash of blades

giggling

Am I exciting you?

clash

teasing Did you want to see my breast bounce as we battle?

clash

Such a primal human beast. Don't think I'll waste MY time cutting off YOUR clothes. Not that you have many. If I get through your guard, I'm going straight for your heart. *giggle* It'll look pretty in a jar on my shelf, won't it?

clashing

breathless You are really surprisingly good at this. Who trained you? Where did you learn to fight this way? Some of these moves, I haven't seen them before. That one was like a wolf flickering in the shadows, and that parry was like a rhino lifting its horn. It's really quite wonderful. I want to know who taught you!

gasps

You … cut away my top from my other shoulder!

Well.

Here are my breasts. Naked and sweet and swollen and ready to be touched. Mmm, maybe I'll touch them and give myself pleasure, after I've cut out your heart. You ARE good at this. Exciting, really.

clashing

And I confess a little of my warm elven honey IS trickling down my thighs, under my tight battle-skirt. I haven't had a duel this exhilarating in two hundred years. I am SO glad they sent you.

Before you die, you MUST tell me who taught you.

clashing

That's it. Watch my breasts dance as I move. Watch my tits. Not my blades.

giggling Be distracted, mortal invader!

clashing

panting a little

All right, I … don't seem to be able to get past your guard at all. How is that possible? I'm actually pressed.

clashing

panting with exertion

Pressing your advantage? Forcing me back toward the window? That won't do.

clashing

Ha! A cut right across your hip. *panting* Yes, I know it's barely a scratch, but it burns a little, doesn't it? Oh, give me something, you muscled barbarian. I'm used to leaving an opponent in pieces by now. At least be good-natured about it and wince or whimper a little.

grunting in exertion as the swords clash

It's like fighting a giant. Or a rockface. *worried* It's a good thing I'm good at this.

clashing

Ohh…okay … the windowsill. *whimpers* My hips are on the windowsill. The night air at my back. Well, that's not good. Really, really not good. Mmm, though the music outside DOES sound lovely. My people are dancing beneath the willows. Not as sweaty and hot as I am dancing, but …

clashing, and one of her blades flies from her hand

gasps You've sent one of my blades flying, out the window! Oh, the arc it makes in the starlight, flashing through the air—that IS pretty.

clashing

I … I can't … move you. *panting*

Oh, you like what my tits are doing as I pant? You like the sweat trickling down between my breasts?

out of breath You really AREN'T going to win, you know. I MUST defend the queen!

clashing blades

a little cry

You!!! You human savage! You've … you've cut open my battle-skirt! And bared my naked elven pussy! You beast. *she gives a little scream* Die, human!

clashing of blades

her furious little grunts as she fights him

then her startled cry

All right, barbarian warrior. *panting* All right, all right. You have my blade pinned to the sill. Your hand at my throat. *her breaths come in quick little gasps* You could take away my breath with a squeeze of your fingers. Or you could push me over the windowsill.

I shudder to admit it, but you have bested me. At least momentarily. I don't know quite how you did it.

I'll ... let go ... of my blade.

it clatters

softly Do not hurt me, human. You and I, let's talk. You have time to talk, don't you? I won't cry out. No one would hear me; all the other elves are at the holy dance, and the queen is sleeping just through that door and you have all night to do whatever heinous things you came here to do to her.

So, delay a moment, warrior, and let's ... talk. Mmm, about your intentions.

What are you going to do with Nikaia of the elves, with Nikaia of the blades?

You have me completely naked. Tattooed and hot and helpless. My battle skirt in a pool about my feet. My breasts heaving. My soft elven lips ... parted. Strands of my hair sweaty across my face. My thighs ... look. *whispers* Just look. My thighs are such ... soft ... cream.

breathing hard How your eyes burn above mine.

Are you really going to tip me out this window? To watch my beautiful elven body fall to the street far below? Is that REALLY what you're going to do with your vanquished elfgirl? Slay her?

he kisses her, fierce and passionate

she moans sweetly into the kiss

Mmmmm. That's a better idea. But you call that a kiss, human? THIS is a kiss.

kissing

the kiss is long and sensual and heated

it is so long and so hot, it goes on, and she maons into his mouth, muffled and hungry

breathless after That ... is how you kiss an elfgirl.

gasps You're parting my thighs. *moans* Forcing your hips between my legs. *gaspy and aroused* Are you going to ravage me, right on this windowsill? Where I dare not squirm or struggle for fear of falling? Is that what you came here for, human? To fuck an elfgirl? While my tits heave and my pussy tightens and my eyes shine in the starlight?

fierce and sultry Let the queen sleep and dream her dreams of empire, human boy. My cunt will clench your cock as tight as hers. I'll show you.

moans Mmmn, your hands. That's it, mortal. You like having your hands on my elven tits? *aroused* My nipples swell and harden more than a human girl's. Pinch them, warrior. Mmmn! I was going to cut out your heart. *moans* Press your advantage, you masculine beast. Pinch my nipples. Squeeze my tits. *moans*

You must have fantasized about this often in your primitive human war-camp, while you tossed and writhed in your bedding. So many nights, you must have imagined pinning a captured elfgirl under you, covering her mouth, making her squeal into your hand as you forced pleasure on her. Show me what you fantasized about, you rugged brute. What does a human barbarian dream of doing to an elfgirl's hot, full tits?

squeals

You bit me!

panting desperately

squeals again

You dreamed of BITING my tits?!

whimpers of arousal All right, human. Bite me! Bite my tits!

moaning and gasping

Be savage to me! Like a wolf to his mate! Mark my sensitive elven flesh! *moans*

whispers hotly You've bested me. Claim your spoils, warrior.

a sudden cry

Your fingers … inside me! You brute! I am small and tight! Mortal!

her moans and squeals

I'm squirming against your hand! Slick and hot. Flooding your hand with my nectar. *panting* What you're doing to me! You beast.

Kiss me, you animal. Kiss me and fuck me with those fingers. Mmmphh!

grunting and whimpering helplessly against his mouth as he kisses her

we hear the rustling of the human warrior's garments

she whimpers against his mouth

panting You've bared your cock! You've taken out your cock! *flustered and hot* You really mean to do this to me. You're going to fuck me. You're going to fuck me with that hard human cock!

low and sultry With this cock. Oh, feel my fingers curl around it … *whispers* oh, so big.

How you throb in my hand.

So warm.

You REALLY want to ravish me.

Do it, then.

growls Do it. I will defend the queen. Take me instead. *moans* Ravage me, human. Fuck me.

beside herself with arousal Here, right here. This is my tight heat. Right here. This small, wet opening. *whispers* You can take it. Take me, mortal. Push your cock inside me.

whimpering with need I'll let go of your cock. Wrap my arms around you, my fingers clutching at your shoulders. Hold my hips when you thrust in me, human. Do NOT drop me into the street below. Do not. Oh, fuck. I can feel that brutal human cock rubbing against my tight pussy. Oh, human. Human. *moans* Hold me tight and don't drop me, and I promise I'll squirm so well for you. Wet and wriggling in your arms. *panting* Kiss my tits and fuck me. Fuck your elf-captive by starlight.

she cries out as he enters her

a few breathless squeals as she tries to take him, his girth, his roughness

panting You're going to tear me apart, human!

passionate grunts and moans for a few moments as they fuck

You're stretching me! I'm so … SO tight! Unnh! Unnh! Unnh! Feel me cling to your shoulders and rock my hips, oh yes, yes, yes, unnh, unnh, unnh, fucking RAVAGE me, human! Unnh! Unnh! I could have slain you! Unnh! Now FUCK me until I'm a soaked, sweaty, whimpering mess! Unnh! Unnh! Come ON! FUCK ME! Harder! Unnh! Unnh!

her passionate grunts

a SQUEAL

Oh, how you SINK that cock in me! Oh my GODDESS! YES!

panting

You take this cunt, warrior. You take this hot elven cunt! I am Nikaia of the elves! Take it, mortal! Take what you want! Fuck me! Warrior, GIVE. ME. PLEASURE! *cries of pleasure* Feel me squeeze and … ohh! yes! … I'll swirl my hips … *panting* … more, more, more …

Oh yes, YES, grab my tits! But so help me, mortal, if you spill me out this window, I WILL cut out your heart! Oh GODDESS! Hold me tight!

he covers her mouth with his hand firmly

Mmmph! mmmph!

she cries out into his hand, wildly, passionately, desperately, her elfgirl body on fire with passion and need

a biting sound

moans Yes! I bit your hand! Your hand on my mouth! I bit you! I can bite, too! I can bite. I need to scream, I need to SCREAM!

she does

wailing with pleasure Oh warrior, warrior! Your cock, your cock, your cock! I can't! I can't! WHY did the gods give humans such ... thick ... cocks?!!!

improv intense, passionate sex

Your cock is so beautiful inside me. Your cock is a fucking warrior! Unnh! Unnh! Unnh! It's so hot inside me! So hot! So hot! Oh warrior, warrior, feel my cunt GRIP your cock, yes YES! *squeals* Beautiful male! Hear the music of my people, the dancing elves, hear it, hear it, all of them at the sacred festival, none of them know their quee – *she stops herself from saying it* – their swordswoman, their sweet strong Nikaia, is being FUCKED! *squeals* Oh, your fingers bruise my breasts! Pound me, pound me, pound me! Oh, yes, yes, YES.

wildly Am I everything you dreamed? When you writhed and moaned and fucked your fist, on your bedding, in your barbaric war-camp? Am I as tight, as small, as slick as you dreamed? Oh goddess, I am SOAKED in sweat! I'm going to yield, I'm going to yield and yield and yield! Warrior, have mercy! Don't finish in me! Finish on my tits! Finish on my soft thighs! On my cheeks and chin! Oh, cover me with your semen! Be a barbarian to me and leave me dripping with your hot seed! Just not inside me! Have mercy!

panting What do you mean 'no mercy'? What do you mean 'no mercy'!!! Wait, wait, wait, wait, warrior! Warrior! Not in me! Not in me! Not inside me!!!!! No! You brute!! Wait! Ahhhh!!

she screams in orgasm

a low wail

she barely has any breath

I … I … am clinging. To you. Panting. And sweaty. And so full of your cock.

a whimper of pleasure and shocked realization

You spilled your seed in me, human.

You … animal.

in wonder How could you?

breathless, awed I have been completely … ravaged … by a human warrior.

panting

suddenly a little vulnerable, her voice small Hold me. *whispers* Please.

Hold me.

she makes soft little noises in his arms for a few moments

Such strong, human arms. *whispers* Oh, I can't believe what just happened to me.

Oh, human. Your cock in me is … wonderful.

Beautiful male. Mmmn.

kissing him

soft little noises into the kiss

softly I let you win. You know that, right? *giggles* I hadn't been fucked hard in so long.

And I've never been fucked like THIS.

giggling With my warm elven ass on this windowsill. *breathily* Don't drop me, warrior. Hold me.

kissing

Mmm. I have a … proposition.

Mmm-hmm.

Why don't you take me captive for a few nights? Let the queen sleep in her bedchamber. You can have … me. *giggles* I did squirm well, didn't I?

flustered Why ... why are you laughing?

You ... *squeaks* ... you knew?!!

You knew all along I was the queen of the elves?!

blushing, angry and aroused Do you mean to tell me this whole time, you knew you were ravishing the queen?! That you were making the queen squirm on your cock? You ... you ... beast!

the sound of a blade

haughty, still breathless You may have tossed MY blades aside, but you forgot to watch YOURS. Now it's at your throat, mortal. An elven queen is not like some human princess. *proudly* I am a hot, naked, tattooed battle-elf! With a blade at your throat.

What ... ? I look ... fetching ... with my face flushed in anger, my breasts heaving? *indignant and aroused* Oh!!

I should slit your throat, mortal! You CAME in the queen of the elves. You have NO idea the diplomatic incident THIS is going to cause. Yes, I'm sure assassinating me in my sleep would have been worse, but still.

sighs softly I guess if I do bear a child, I can't exactly execute the child's father. Mmmn. Especially not when he has SUCH a cock. Oh, how your cock throbs in me.

whispers Stop that. Seriously. We have negotiations to do. You can't just fuck me agai- ahhh! Unnh!

growls Oh, you arrogant mortal. *panting* Yes, yes, it's true. My tight elven cunt CRAVES this cock.

a helplessly aroused sound

I came back to the palace alone while my people danced and drummed and fucked to the holy music under the willows, because I was so BORED. You have no idea how BORING it is to be the queen. It's all war councils and disputes over the price of passionfruit, and demanding tribute from sweaty, rebellious humans, and arguments over land, and ceremonies by moonlight and by sunrise, and … taxes. So many taxes. Ugh. And one of my spies told me an assassin might come tonight.

And he DID cum tonight, didn't he? *giggling*

her voice burns with heat I made him cum.

Mmmn, so, once the festival started, I … snuck … back. Looking for a little excitement, a little adventure. *playful* And you certainly delivered the adventure!

giggling Aren't you glad you didn't drop me out the window?

Mmmmn. You know, my people will be dancing all night under the willows. No one's going to find you or think of executing you for at least another seven hours. So. Right over there, through that door, there IS a big bed with satin sheets and a canopy of silk supported on posts of ivory and oak. And … I SHOULD dance tonight. Every elven woman should dance tonight, even the queen. I danced the blades, but I need to dance naked for a male. It pleases the goddess. Mmmn, so why don't I take you to my bed, tie you spread to those posts, dance like you have NEVER seen a woman dance, and fuck you 'til the sun rises?

Or until your hard human cock can't take it anymore. Whichever comes first.

softly A few of these sigils and spells tattooed red on my body aren't for battle. *whispers* They're for fucking.

Mmmn. And once you're exhausted and you're bound and shaking on my bed, I can interrogate you … with kisses … and find out what human chieftain wanted me assassinated tonight. Because that really isn't nice. I don't LIKE being assassinated.

Come on. Take me to bed.

Or we can keep trying to kill each other. Either way. *giggles*

Mmmn. That's my good warrior.

rustling as they get up

moans Oh, I'm so sore. You REALLY fucked me hard. *whimpers* I don't even know if I can walk after that … that massive cock. You humans fuck like gods. It is definitely unfair. *quivers* No one should be able to just destroy an elf queen like this. *whimpers*

in wonder Oh … what's this? Ohhhh, your cum is leaking out of my pussy, warm and sticky down my leg. Mmm. Wow. *moans* I am Nikaia, queen of the elves, and I am dripping human cum down my leg.

Okay, okay. Seven hours til dawn. Don't ... don't try anything, warrior. I still have this big sword. See? Sword. Whoosh!

sound of sword cutting through air

breathless To the bedroom! You're going to tell me EVERYthing about who sent you here, and you're going to fuck me again with that frighteningly thick human cock until I can't even think or breathe or speak. To bed! Or ... wait. Kiss me first. Mmmn, let me press my lithe elven body to you ... my tits against your chest ... my pussy pressed to your thigh. *whispers* This pussy you ravaged.

breathless Kiss me. Kiss me, human.

a deep, sensual kiss

moaning into the kiss

the sword clattering to the ground

breathless I'm disarmed again? Oh, fine. *a sultry, moaning whine of need* Never mind who has captured who. Just take me to bed and fuck me. Take me to bed, warrior! And fuckkk me!

kissing

hungry moans into the kiss

the scene ends

Lust After Battle: Soldier Girls and Swordmaidens

2

Dancing the Blades: Ronin After the Battle

TAGS: [F4M] [Romance] [Confessing Her Love] [Blowjob] [Woman on Top] [Woman in Love] [Passion] [Blowjob After Sex]

a painting I saw inspired me to write this story of a ronin in love with her shogun, waking him with a kiss after defending him on the battlefield

the scene opens after battle, with the swordmaiden strong but pleading for her lord's safety, terrified he might be mortally wounded or dead

My shogun, my lord? Oh, please be all right. Please. Please open your eyes. The battle's over, I saved you. I know I did. Open your eyes, my lord! Please don't be dead. Open your eyes, my lord, my ... my love.

Please be breathing. Let me listen at your lips.

softly If you need my life's breath, you've only to ask. Here ... my love ... let me press my mouth to yours and give you my breath.

she kisses him

whispers Open your eyes. Live.

kissing

a soft gasp You're alive! You're alive! Oh, my lord! It's all right, shhh, you're safe. Don't be scared, my shogun. You're on the battlefield but the battle is done. I've taken off my armor and used it to prop you up so that your head won't rest on the cold ground. This rag barely concealing the swell of my breasts, that and my battle-skirt are all I'm wearing.

No, don't get up. Lie still. Rest. Here, I have a flask at my hip, let me open it and lift it to your lips. It isn't water, my lord, but its fire will fortify you. There, my good lord, drink. *whispers* Please drink. Let me help you be strong again.

That's my good lord. Drink deep.

There.

You're shaking. I fear the blows they gave you. Here, let me hold your head in my lap, smooth the pain from your temples and brow with my fingers. There you go, my lord. Let my touch soothe you, my shogun. Shh, shhh, it's all right. I've got you. There's only us here. Your foes ... *her voice hardens* ... I danced the blades and the earth drinks their blood even now. They will never bother you again.

I told you ... *a catch in her voice* ... when you banished me ... *a little defiantly* that my blade and my body are for your service, my shogun, until my death. I came out of the forest a mere hour ago, at sunset before it got dark, found your samurai slain about you and assassins surrounding you. I saw when the bandit struck you across your head and sent you toppling to the ground like a midwinter tree. And battle rage burned in my blood, and I rushed from the trees at your enemies while the sun burned its way out of the sky. My katana sang in the air.

Yes, there were fourteen of them. And one of me.

proudly They didn't stand even a chance.

her voice trembles with love for him and passion You are safe. I will NEVER let anyone hurt you.

I know. I know I am ronin, my lord. That I am not permitted by your side. Only allow me to stay here until you recover, allow me to help you get back to your house safely. The night is already dark, there may be other assassins about. Banish me at dawn, my lord, if you must. Banish me, but I will still follow you and watch over you and protect you. To be parted from you is death. Send me to a far corner of the world, I will still return and my blade will be there when you need me.

whispers I know you need me.

Your samurai were weak. They were unfit guardians for my lord. They have paid the price for it. But I am not like them, my shogun. I am strong. I will always be strong for you. My body is stronger than a man's, swifter, tougher. My body can withstand the pain of battle and the pain of childbirth. My mind is stronger than a man's, less easily distracted, focused relentlessly on the one goal of keeping my lord alive. *softly* And well. And ... not alone.

My heart is stronger than a man's. *her voice chokes very slightly with emotion* Strong enough even to withstand the pain of banishment. Strong enough to fight for the man I lo... *corrects herself before she can get the word "love" out* ... the man I serve, whatever comes.

Have another drink, my lord.

There. That's it.

We must make YOU strong again.

Do you hear the crickets? And see the stars bursting into flames in the night sky? *fiercely* Fear nothing in this forest, my lord. I will keep you safe tonight. Here, let me set your head back down on my armor. Lie still, my lord, while I make a fire. There is wood enough here to burn.

I'll just gather some of it up... pile it near your side. I'll keep you warm tonight.

I have flint and tinder here...

You're...you're watching me. The way you look at me... Not dismissively, like the last time I saw you, when you sent me away. You're looking at me like ... *quivery* ... What's that in your eyes?

It doesn't matter. I'll get this fire lit and I'll stand watch over you. And if you don't want to look at me, at the warrior you banished, you can close your eyes and I will protect you, unseen, in the dark.

gasps softly My lord? You've taken my wrist.

What… what is it you want to tell me?

short, gasping breaths, struggling for control of her emotions You … you do want to see me? You … you want to see me always at your side? My shogun? Defending you always, with my blade and my body *whispers* and my life?

Are you … *trembly, holding back her fear that he might be* … are you mocking me?

angry and vulnerable, relating her greatest shame, near to tears but refusing to cry You sent me away. Like … like you were ashamed of me. You said you would not be the one shogun in the land to be so feeble that he must be defended by … by a woman. And now you … now you want …

listens, then repeats his words in wonder You … you were wrong?

whispers Wrong?

softly It's … nothing. I just … I just am not used to hearing a man say he was wrong. It's not something you men usually do.

I … I like hearing it.

optional sound effect at this point and throughout the rest of the script: the quiet crackle of a wood fire

There, the fire's lit. And I'll keep it ted. It's a very pleasing fire; I do good work. Turn your face toward it, my lord. Let it warm you.

You WERE wrong, you know. If not for me, you'd be in several pieces now. *a little proudly* I wish you could have seen me fight. The slash and spin of my blade, the flash of my thighs, the dance of my body over the grass. I fought like a goddess for you.

W…why? What do you mean, 'why'?

You're my shogun.

I'm your … I WAS your samurai. I fight for you. It's what I do.

Yes, I know I didn't need to. Being ronin. But … I … I wouldn't … *a low growl* … oh why is it so hard to speak? I've never had trouble speaking before. It's only that what I have to say is buried deep in my heart like a cherry tree seed waiting through the winter for the sun's warmth, and now … and now I see … warmth … in your eyes, and everything is cracking inside me and bursting green out of my heart and pushing up through my throat like a sprouting plant and it's choking all my words. I need words. I need … I need some way to say I love you.

gasps, shocked at herself

I…

quivers … I am so sorry.

I … I didn't mean to say that. Or I did. I didn't. I don't know.

I meant no dishonor to you. I'm sorry.

talking quickly I … I will see you safe home in the morning and go away into the trees after, and you will never have to see my face again, though I will watch you and guard you and give my life for you and …

he interrupts her

You …

you don't mind? That I … that I love you?

trembling My lord … what do you mean?

listens

You accept my love? *almost tearful as she repeats the words he has given her* … More than any shogun has ever accepted his warrior's love and loyalty? More than any man has ever wanted his woman's heart, you … you want mine?

almost a squeak What do you mean, that's why you sent me away?

Because you loved me?

You … *amazed* … you banished me from your side because you LOVED me?

You … you … *searching for a word* … oh, so like a man!

Let me lean over you close, I need to see your eyes, I need to see the truth in them, because if you're mocking me now I swear I will die, I will not live til the morn-mmmmphhhhhhh

he interrupts her with a kiss

she protests weakly into the kiss, then surrenders in soft, soft muffled moans gasping You ... you kissed me?

another kiss, longer

whispery My lord! Do you ... do you love me?

I ... I have dreamed of kissing you, every night since I was a girl. Every night I've dreamed of your touch, with my hand between my soft thighs. With your name on my lips, ... your NAME, my lord, as though I was your wife or your lover and not your blade and your warrior. *softly* I've dreamed of kissing you.

Let me cup your face in my hands, my fingers gentle as a mother with a baby, and I'll kiss you again, my love.

kissing

I want to kiss you until I haven't air left to breathe.

kissing... a long, sensual, passionate kiss

breathing fast Yes, my lord, yes, slip your hand under the rag around my breasts, just like that. *moans softly* Your warm hand cupping my breast. My breasts are so sensitive in the night air, and my nipples swell at your touch. *whispers* Do you feel my warmth under your fingers? Do you feel my heartbeat? I want you to feel the thunder of my heart for you while we kiss.

kissing him

Here, let me tug your shirt open as well. I want to feel the warmth of your body. When I saw you lying on the ground and feared you were dead ... the thought of you cold, oh my lord, the thought of that destroyed me. And here you are, by the fire I've lit, with another fire I've lit in your eyes… warm … as I swing my leg over you and straddle you … your chest so warm under my hands, your hips warm between my thighs. I saved you. And you are so full of life.

softly Do you feel my breast?

softer than before, almost a whisper Do you feel my heartbeat?

I burn for you, my love. My heart and my body are FIRE at your touch.

I need to touch you, too.

No, you lie still while I unfasten the rest of your garments. You lie still. You don't GET to tell me you love me and then be shy. If you reject me now you'll break me into a thousand pieces, like a sword against the wall of a cliff. Don't you DARE. I am giving you my heart. Don't you dare break it.

I am going to ride you and make love to you by this fire and keep you warm and safe all night, and in the morning, you will either reject me and I will pursue you through every dark forest in this world, your ronin, and wherever you go my blade will flicker about you and cut apart any assassin or thief who will ever trouble you … or … or you will take me as your wife. You are a man of honor. I know what you will choose.

I know what you've already chosen. Look how hard you are when I take you in my hand. Your cock is like a thousand-year tree, like an undefeated warrior, powerful and strong.

Your cock is hard for me, my love. *whispers* And I am so wet for you.

I have been dripping down my thighs under this battleskirt since you kissed me.

whispers I want you in me.

Lie back.

Shhh. Lie still, my love.

I have one more battle to win tonight.

Shhh… feel my hand pressing down on your chest, holding you there while I kiss … *kissing* … my way down your belly … *kissing* … and lick gently at your thighs … *licking sounds*

a soft, moaning sigh

My lord, the way you smell. Like such a man… And the softness of your balls against my cheek.

licking gently

No, lie still. Lie still. *fiercely* You are mine, whether you banish me or no. You said you LOVE me, and you are mine tonight.

quivery I love you. I would burn the world to protect you.

My body burns for you already.

Let me do this, my shogun. Let me close my mouth hot and wet around your cock …

gentle, passionate blowjob sounds

mmmm mmmm that's my lord ... mmm mmmmm ... fill my mouth ... mmmmm ... I'm going to show you how I love you, my shogun, my beautiful man ... mmm mmmm

improv a sensual, passionate blowjob

Did you ever imagine this, my lord? That I would be pleasing you with my mouth by a warm woodfire after saving your life in battle?

sucking gently

I have dreamed of this so many times.

Yet I never knew how warm and firm your cock would feel on my tongue ... how good you would taste in my mouth ...

sucking

whispers I'll caress your balls with my fingers

sucking ... moaning around his cock

Oh, how your thighs tremble when I do that.

moaning louder, muffled, around his cock

I love how your thighs quiver for me, my love.

sucking and moaning around his cock

I love you.

sucking I love you.

sucking You feel so hot in my mouth.

whispers I want to try something.

she takes him into her throat ... gagging sweetly but continuing ... after a little while, she lifts her mouth from him, panting

All right. I think you're more than hard enough.

breathless

For what? ... For this.

For me, straddling you. My battleskirt settling around your hips like a blanket.

For me, ahhhhhhh ... sliding my soft, wet folds along your cock.

whispers Oh, I'm so wet. So slick and wet.

I've never been this wet, my love. Only for you. Only for you.

Ah! Oh! At my entrance. Here, let me press my breasts to your chest, take your face in my hands ... I want to kiss the man I love while I take him inside me for the first time.

kissing, deep sensual kissing ... then her muffled cry as she sinks down on his cock without breaking the kiss... and her muffled moans

wet sounds

she lifts her lips from his, gasping You feel so good in me! You feel so good!

kissing You're so thick! *kissing, moaning, breathless* Feel me ride you *kissing* Ohhh!!!! Rolling my hips.

Like a geisha, you say? Oh you beast of a man. My body KNOWS how to dance. *kissing* I have danced the blades. *kissing* I have balanced in the treetops while marauders approached below like ignorant prey. *kissing* I can pivot on a toe and take a man through the heart. *kissing* This, this rolling and swiveling of my hips, this is nothing, my lord. Not yet. Let me show you how I can REALLY dance. I am going to show you what a warrior a woman can be. I'll show how a woman overcomes a man when she has his heart!

panting, her moans and wet sounds intensify, the sex fast and desperate and passionate

Yes! Yes! Get your hands on my breasts! *panting* How you throb in me when I grip and ripple around your cock! Kiss my nipples!

moaning

Your mouth on my breasts! Oh, my shogun! My love! You are so thick in me! So big!

moaning I love your cock in me! I love riding you! With you glistening with sweat beneath me and the fire in your eyes! Ohh, put your hands on my hips, I want your hands all over me. Love me, you foolish, wonderful man. *crying out* Oh you feel so GOOD!

Yes, my nails are digging into your shoulders. I'm sorry. You're going to need to hurt for me a little, my lord. I can't hold back, I've burned for you in secret so long. I've waited for you all my life, since I was a girl, since I first saw you in your house among all your samurai, your warriors so tall and proud. I yearned so to be one of them, to be forever at your side, defending you against all the world, against demon and dark undead and outlaw and rebel, dancing my blade to earn one approving glance from those deep eyes of yours.

Those deep eyes that are SO approving right now.

My shogun, my shogun, ohhhhh, listen to the music our bodies make! Listen to me riding you! Our thighs slapping together! I love you! I love you!

Ahhh! Feel me grip your cock, so tight! I feel you so DEEP in me! Give me the joy I seek, my lord! Make me cum! Make me cum for the man I love! Yes! Yes! Your fingers on my clit. Yes! Yes! Yes! Feel me clenching! I love you! I love you! I've always loved you!

her wild, passionate orgasm, crying out "I love you!" as she cums

quivering afterward

whispers I didn't know it would feel so wonderful.

I can tell you're close, too. Here, let me lift myself from you ... *moans as his cock leaves her* ... and I will take your cock in my soft, wet mouth.

giggles You have battled so hard to hold back your pleasure, to give me that orgasm that just shook me like a leaf in autumn. You MUST love me, then.

My dear lord. You have fought with honor, my love. But I WILL vanquish you, as surely as I did all your foes.

YOU I will defeat with my soft … wet tongue … *licking* … with my warm breath across the tip of your cock … *her soft sigh of breath, exhaling across his cock* … with my gentle, loving mouth…

sucking him

You WILL cum in my mouth, my love.

sucking

I want your seed in my mouth.

improv the sounds of a sensual, urgent blowjob, wet and hot

gasping between sucking his cock Finish in my mouth, my lord. Mmmmm mmmmm Here by the fire mmmm mmmm mmmm Give me your cum mmmm mmmm I want to swallow it for you mmm mmmmm I want your cock to pulse in my mouth mmmmm mmmm Surrender to me, my love mmmm mmmm Just let go mmmm mmmmm Let go mmmm mmm surrender, my love, yield to me mmmm mmmmmm Cum for me mmm mmmm Cum for me mmmmmm I love you mmmmm

muffled around his cock Cum in my mouth … cum in my mouth … cum in my mouth …

her triumphant moan as he spasms in her mouth … then the sounds of her swallowing a few times breathless Oh my love. My love. My thighs are still trembling. Yours too.

I'll slip into your arms by this fire with my pussy hot and soaked against your thigh and my breasts ... ahhhh!!!!!! ... soft and sensitive in your strong hands ... *moans* ... and I'll kiss your neck, my love ... *kissing him* ... *a series of soft, gentle kisses on his neck*

Mmmmm. Yes, I'm caressing you, one hand cupping your warm balls, one hand caressing your beautiful face, ohhh, even as you caress me. My love. My lord. You felt wonderful inside me.

Mmmm. Hold me. And listen to the fire.

softly I like the sound of the fire. I like how it sounds after I've fucked the man I love.

shyly Will you keep me with you tomorrow? *whispers* And ... not banish me? I don't want to be ronin anymore. I want to be yours. I want you to be mine.

breathless with love when she hears his answer Domo arigato. *kissing*

whispers I'm so happy.

speaking with all the love in her heart My blade and my body are for your service, my shogun, every night until my last breath. I will never leave you, nor permit any warrior to ever take you from me. Our hearts beat as one, even as they did when I came clenching around your cock. And no one will spill your heart's blood unless they first drench this earth in mine.

kissing

And that will never happen.

My foolish, wonderful man. *kissing* Your heart and your body are mine to protect.

kissing

And I can dance the blades better than any man in the world.

kissing

her voice quivering with passion And I love you. I love you!

Now rest, my lord, my love. Rest. I'll see you safely home when the sun rises. Tonight, I will keep watch. And when I am sure the night is silent and safe … *softly* … I will wake you gently and make love to you again.

I'll grip your cock and make you yield to me, again and again. I'll make you scream with pleasure, my shogun. We'll scream together, you and me. We'll wake the whole world together.

Rest now, my lord. *so softly* I love you.

the scene ends with a slow, gentle kiss

Lust After Battle: Soldier Girls and Swordmaidens

Sergeant Ashley Stargun, Third Earth Army,
meeting you in your dreams each night

3

My Beautiful Warrior

TAGS: [F4M] [Fellow Soldiers] [Kissing] [Passion] [Desperate] [Here, Keep My Tits Warm] [These are Army Tits] [Woman of Your Dreams, Literally, Rescuing You Each Night] [Begging] [Cowgirl] [Fuck Me Like You Mean It, Soldier!] [Creampie]

There is wind. We hear distant gunfire, the roar of descending dropships, and then, nearer, the tread of combat boots over loose gravel. A little distance away, the radio at the woman's belt crackles. Then a woman's voice over the radio says, "They're flanking us. Get that artillery up!"

the footsteps stop once they get close.

Do you hear the wind, soldier? It's always so cold here, on this planet. Every time we drop.

a soft, amused sound No, you've made this drop before. You just don't remember. But never mind that now. *a sigh* What have they done to you, soldier? Scorch marks on the right side of your face, that wound in your side.

a catch in her breath

You're dying. *softly* I'm so sorry. I tried to get here in time, but…

the sounds of gravel as she crouches

Let me take a look. Here, shhh, shhh, it's okay. It's okay. I'll cup your cheek in my hand. Oh, my beautiful warrior. Do you think you can stand?

Oh no. No, no-no-no. Here, let me get … *grunts* … my shoulder under your arm. Fuck, I forget how BIG you are. Shh, shh, it's all right. I didn't get to be sergeant by being weak. I can carry your weight. Come on. Let's get you up that ridge before we're surrounded.

breathing heavily

footsteps in gravel

Got separated from my squad. If we can get to another alpha drop squad and find you a medic …

angry No, that's enough of THAT talk, soldier. You are NOT laying back down. Just one foot in front of the other. *devoted, passionate* I'm going to save you.

No, I don't think we've stopped the planetkiller yet. This side of the ridge, we're badly outnumbered. Your pod wasn't the only one they shot out of the air. That was a BAD landing. Come on. Come on.

footsteps

she's panting

Yeah, I know, sky's all full of colors. That's their fucking ordnance.

gunfire is getting closer

Shit. Come on, there's a downed ship over there. If we can get to the other side of it, it might block us from view for the first part of the climb. Come on. March, soldier! I swear to God, I am getting you home this time.

What's that? *panting* Don't you remember my name?

softly Please tell me you remember.

whispers Fuck.

It's Ashley. Sergeant Ashley Stargun. Five hundred and seventeen drops and you STILL can't remember my name. I should be insulted.

Never mind. Come on, just … have to get you … over this debris …

gunfire, close

her radio crackles: "Alpha squads, alpha squads, regroup at coordinates 009 73. Double time it! Move, move!"

Shit!

more gunfire

Here, just a moment, let me … let me lean you against this hull. Some cover, at least.

rustling and gravel as she sets him down

There. Breathe. I'll be right back. I'm just going to stand up. Get my binocs out, scan that field of debris in our way. Need to know what we're up against.

You're ... staring at my ass, aren't you? Well, you do that. If blood's flowing to your cock, that means you're still alive, right? Here, watch my ass. I'll get a look at the terrain and you ... you get a good look, too.

Huh. Huh. Well, THAT's not good.

whispers Shit. Shit-shit-shit.

gunfire, closer

she throws herself down beside him

Shit, shit, shit. Okay, Ashley, think. Think-think-think.

panting I think we're cut off. There's a whole battalion moving across the slope, over there. You can't see them with the ship's wing in the way, but the moment we pop out, they'll spot US. And behind us, they've got hunter squads closing in. Maybe seven, eight. Twenty men each. It's not good.

I ... *almost tearful* ... shit!

breathing heavily for a moment

Okay, well, we aren't going anywhere. Let's get you bandaged up better. Yeah. I don't have a medic kit but ... here ...

sound of a zipper

rustling clothes

What am I doing? What does it look like I'm doing, soldier? Getting naked. My drop jacket should make a good bandage, don't you think?

more rustling

No, no bra. Never wear one to battle. Bad luck. Yeah, that's all right, soldier. You just ... um ... you just get a good hot look at my tits while I wrap this around your side ...

rustling

... cinch it tight ...

There. What do you think? Not exactly regulation-issue medical care, but it will do. *a soft, amused sound* You're ... still staring at my tits.

softly That's ... that's all right. You can ... you can touch them.

No, do.

I ... I can see your eyes, silly man. And your combat fatigues aren't doing shit to hide that bulge at your groin. Go ahead. *softly* If you want to.

whispers Touch my tits.

Mmmn.

she moans very softly

Ohh. I ... keep forgetting how ... good ... your hands are. Mmmn.

Do you like that? My nipples like hard berries against your palms?

soft, sweet sounds from her

Mmn. You feel like you're dreaming? Funny you should mention that ...

Ooooh!

Ooh, yeah, that's ... that's okay. You can be rough. My tits can take it. These are army tits. They've seen a lot of battles.

moans

breathless There. Feel more alive now? Good.

Listen. I ... I don't think we're making it out this time. The hunter squads will be converging on us in ... I don't know. Ten minutes. Maybe less. No, shhh. Shh. Keep your hands on my tits. It ... I feel warmer with them there. This wind is making goosebumps all over me. *softly* Keep my tits warm.

Mmn.

Keep me warm.

getting emotional And listen. Listen to your Ashley.

Listen, soldier. I ... I thought ... *trembling* ... I really thought I could save you this time. I thought ...

No! No, I'm not crying. Don't be absurd. I'm the sergeant of an alpha squad; we don't cry. There's just so much fucking dust in this wind. Listen. There's not much time. Do you … do you really not remember me?

Even a little?

quivers Do you not remember how I moan when you touch me?

Moans

Look up from my tits a second. My eyes. Look at my eyes, soldier. I never look the same, one battle to the next, but my eyes. My eyes are always the same. My eyes are always full of … Just look at my eyes.

tearful You know me.

Please.

so, so softly Tell me you know me.

Before they get us, you have to remember. You HAVE to. Dammit, here.

she kisses him, fiercely, passionately, open-mouthed, without restraint, kissing him hot as fire, moaning into his mouth

breathless Fuck, I love how you kiss.

kissing him

You don't remember kissing me before? *Fiercely* I don't believe you.

she kisses him more hotly, desperately

the kiss is long

we hear gunfire, and she whimpers into his mouth but keeps kissing him

panting after the kiss

Yes, I know the enemy is close. Fuck them. Just squeeze my tits and look in my eyes and LISTEN. None of this matters. You understand? None of this. The battle, your orbital pod getting shot down, the planetkiller weapon we were sent to destroy, the hunter squads that are about to come around that edge of that ship and riddle us with bullets. None of it matters. Here … grip my tits. Hard. Make me FEEL it. This is what matters. You and I, we're the only things here that are REAL. You are dreaming. Do you get that? Every night, we crash on this godforsaken planet together and I come find you, and I bind your wounds until my tits are fucking freezing in this cold wind, and each night I try to save you. I have tried so many times to save you. And you have to remember me. You have to. Please remember me. Please. When you wake up, if you remember me, maybe … *holding back tears* … maybe you'll recognize me the next night. Except I never have the same form. My body, my hair, everything changes each time you dream. But my eyes. Remember my eyes. My beautiful warrior, remember my eyes.

her voice trembles with passion And this. Remember this.

she kisses him again, ferociously, mewling into his mouth as they kiss the sound of a zipper

whispers God, this cock. This beautiful cock. *whispers* Sorry my hands are cold. But I know JUST where to put your cock to warm it up.

kissing

whispers Shut up. Shut up, shut up, shut up. Just shut up and kiss me. Breathe in the scent of me. Forget the gunfire and the wind and everything but my body. Please, please, please. Get that cock inside me and kiss me and REMEMBER me.

Feel my fingers so sweet around your cock. Oh, this cock.

kissing him

whispers Do me.

moans Squeeze my tits. *moans* Oh yes, yes.

I lo- Fuck. Fuck. I'm not going to say that, I'm not. *tearful* I CAN'T say those words and lose you again, I can't, I can't, I can't.

she kisses him again

her kiss is wild, needy, desperate

rustling as she gets her uniform out of the way

There, let me straddle you and … yes, yes. There, feel? Feel my soft, tight pussy … right up against your cock. Oh fuck, oh fuck, I'm wet. *breathing fast* I'm going to guide you inside me, soldier. We only have moments. Think you can be fast? Can you fuck me fast and cum in me? Let me grip your hair.

kissing him hotly

low and breathy I need your cum in me.

I want to be leaking your cum down my thighs when I come find you in your dreams tomorrow.

You have a really good cock, and I have a really good pussy, and I'm going to ride you, soldier. *emotional* I'm going to ride you so hard you'll never forget.

Here. Right here. I want your cock … right … here … ah-UHHH!

a squeal as he enters her

That's right. Just like that. Just like that. I'm going to slide down your cock… *moans* … Oh fuck. This cock. Oh … ohhh … my beautiful warrior … let me rock and swivel my hips … grip your arms with my fingers, and … unnh … unnh …

whispers, slow and heated Fuck me.

Oh God, fuck me.

Fuck me, soldier. Fuck me til I scream.

moaning No, it doesn't matter if the enemy hears us. They'll be here any minute. I don't care. I don't care! Just fuck me, just fuck me, fuck me! Please, God, cum in me! I need you! I need you! I need your cum! I need to be so full of you! Please give it to me, give me everything, don't hold back! You are the most beautiful man I've ever met, your body, your heart, please, just please please fill me before you wake! Unnh! Unnh! Unnh! If I'm going to get fucking shot, I want to die full of your cum! Fill me!

kissing him hard, moaning into his mouth

Yes, I know, I know, I'm scratching up your arms, your chest, making you bleed. I'm wild. I'm a sergeant of an alpha squad and I sure as hell fuck like one. And FUCK your cock feels good in me! So thick! So thick! unnh! Unnh! Unnh! That's it, that's it! Fuckkk!

Yes, grip my ass, pull me down onto that cock! Fuck me like you mean it, soldier! Unnh! Unnh! Unnh! Kiss my tits! Mmmn! Mmnn! Bite my tits! Fuck, yes! Fuck! Fuck!

she is a panting, wild mess, moaning and mewling as she rides him

Feel me grip … and squeeze … and milk your cock. I'm going to milk all the cum out of this beautiful cock! You cum in me before you wake, soldier! Don't you dare wake before cumming in me! Cum in me! Cum in me! Cum in me! Do it! Do it! Please, please! *panting wildly* Cum in me, cum in me, cum inside me, please, please cum with me, please cum with me! Ahh! Ahhh!

she orgasms, wild and intense

she is left panting and almost sobbing from pleasure

she kisses him, hotly, breathlessly, mewling sweetly into his mouth

panting Oh my GOD how you throb in me. That is the best thing. That is literally the best thing.

breathless My beautiful warrior. My beautiful warrior.

No, don't look at the soldiers coming around the ship. Yeah, I know. They're going to shoot us. Ignore them. They're not real. Shh, shhh. They're not real. *so softly* My tits are real. My cunt is real. Your cum hot and sticky inside me is real. You're real, and I'm going to find you tomorrow night. I promise. I promise. *tearful* No matter how many times you forget me, I will find you again. *whispers* I will save you.

whispers You came in me.

I can't bear to say goodbye again.

gunfire

whispers Shit.

Here. I'll take your face in my hands. Hold my tits. Look in my eyes. Feel my cunt squeeze ... ahh ... and squeeze ... unnh ... your cock. Listen. Listen. I am Sergeant Ashley Stargun. *so tenderly* I'm Ashley. Remember me.

softly Please remember me.

more gunfire

It's time to wake up. Here ... *whispers* ... My mouth is real. And forever yours. Kiss me. *sniffles* Goodbye, my beautiful warrior. Until you dream of me again.

Kiss me.

whispers Kiss me, soldier.

she kisses him, so sweetly and longingly, making the softest sound into his mouth as she kisses him

the scene ends

4

Succubus Resistance Training, the Night Before Battle on the Plains of Hell

There's a hot fellow soldier (or is she really a succubus infiltrator?) who is concerned that you are not fully prepared to face succubi in battle on the plains of lust and fire tomorrow, and she plans to do something about that.

> TAGS: [F4M] [Seduction] [Wiles] Some [Fsub] and some [FDom] [Training the New Soldier to Resist] [Teasing] [Handjob] [Blowjob] [Passionate Sex] [Virgin Listener] [Fellow Soldier, or Succubus?]

the sound of a fire crackling

gasps, frightened Who goes there?!

Oh. *breathes a sigh of relief* It's you. You're one of the new recruits, aren't you? Yes, go ahead, sit here and warm yourself by my fire. *pauses* Wait, what happened to YOUR fire?

Oh, you lost your gear during the drop?

amused Well, THAT wasn't smart. You really ARE green at this, aren't you? How many drops into the hell plains have you done?

Wait, are you serious?

One?

Including this one?

Holy Michael. Well, I … I guess we did lose a lot of good men at the last battle. A few good women too. We've … sort of been burning through our troops. So, we're down to the greenest replacements now? That's … that's scary.

brightens But this is the final push! If we can just make it across the plain and establish a beachhead on the Magma Sea, we can assault Devil's Fortress itself! It's right there, you can see its dark towers on the horizon, outlined against the volcanic fires. It is literally within our reach!

We just have to push on a few more weeks. We can do it.

giggles I guess I don't need to sound like a recruitment video to you, do I? You're sold. You're already here.

softly I wonder what it will be like when we reach Devil's Fortress. I don't know about you, but I can't stop thinking about it. They say the road is flanked with living sculptures, the captives of the hell plains. On one side of the road, women bound screaming in torment, and on the other side, women bound screaming in lust. For eternity. And once you enter the fortress, the Dark Queen herself, tall as a warship, sits atop a vast throne that is held up on the shoulders of a thousand enslaved men whose souls have been devoured. They stand with their cocks hard as stone, moaning with a need that is never, ever quenched. They say that as you approach the Dark Queen's throne, you feel heat between your thighs like no mortal can bear, and you are stolen from yourself forever.

giggles But soon we'll get there and we'll tear it all down! *cheerful* We're going to win.

Here, scoot closer to the fire. It's going to be a long night, and cold. Brrr! You wouldn't think it, seeing those volcanic fires on the horizon and smelling the sulphur on the night air, but … it's really COLD down here. Even under this uniform, my nipples are hard as little gems right now. *a soft, aroused little whimper*

… Yes, that's right. The major thinks they'll send us in at dawn. Oh, you're … *surprised* you're trembling. Are … are you frightened? Oh god, you're so pale! Oh no, I didn't mean to scare you with all that talk about Devil's Fortress. Oh no. Come here, soldier. Come on. Mmm, yes, here. I'll hold you.

Shhh, shhh, I've got you. I've got you, it's okay. Feel my arms around you. Shh.

We soldiers of the Upper Worlds have to stick together, down here in the nightmare lands.

You've … never charged a line of succubi before, have you? But … you do know what to expect, right? They've briefed you?

… Really? That's … that's all they told you? That's awful.

I was MUCH better trained. No, no, don't feel bad. It's okay. There probably wasn't time. We needed replacements and FAST. But … they can't send you out there tomorrow like this! You poor boy.

Um, well. *sudden resolve as she makes a decision* Okay, listen. We're the only sentries posted this side of the ridge, so … I guess it's private enough to do a quick lesson … to supplement your training. You're going to need it. *softly* No, it's okay. I'm happy to help. I don't want you to fall prey to some lusty devil-girl tomorrow. I HAVE to help. You're one of my war-brothers! We're in the same regiment. We all have to be ready together. It could be MY life you're saving tomorrow in the heat and sweat and excitement of battle, who knows? What kind of soldier would I be, if I didn't help?

Okay, listen. The main thing you have to remember, soldier, is that when you're out there tomorrow walking between pillars of lava and over lakes of volcanic glass, and a succubus, or two, or three, approach you, don't look in their eyes. I mean, a body is just a body, after all. Even if it's a very bosomy and voluptuous body. But a succubus's real powers of seduction are in her eyes. And in her lips. So, try not to look at their faces. That's how they get you. It's how the incubi come after US, too.

What do I mean? Well, here, let me turn so you can see my face better in the firelight. There. Now, see how it appears like I'm glancing down shyly, but I'm actually gazing at you through my eyelashes? See how my gaze goes all hot … and sensual? Like I'm inviting you to kiss me ... to touch me ... to take me? *quivery with arousal* And watch how I part my lips just a little, like this, as if to welcome your cock into my warm, wet little mouth? Mmm-hmm. See? Succubus.

Never look at the eyes. Or lips. So ... so dangerous.

Oh, and you have to watch out for succubi in military uniform. They do that, sometimes: Impersonate us. *giggle* Sometimes they even slip RIGHT into the camp. Scary. So, they could be wearing a uniform, like this one, like mine. How ... how will you know it's one of them? Well, by how they act. Here, I'll show you. You might see her across the lava plain with her back to you. But as you approach, she'll turn slightly and glance at you over her shoulder, like this. With her eyes all smoky and passionate. *softly* Like ... this.

she speaks slowly and seductively And then, when you're captured by her eyes ... yes, just like you're captured by mine right now, mmmm, I can tell by the way you're gazing at me so, so hungrily, *a soft, aroused little noise* ... when she has your attention, she might slip her jacket back to bare one shoulder, like this. See my sleek, beautiful shoulder, warm in the firelight? She'll want to tease you with her soft, feminine flesh. She'll want you thinking about how it will feel when you kiss her shoulder, when you get your mouth on her neck, her breasts. She'll want you to think about your hands on her. So she might let her jacket slip down further. Down her arms, like this. Then she'll turn her body to you, like this, mmmmm, and you'll find out she's unzipped her battle shirt, all the way down to her navel, just like I have, secretly, when you were looking at my eyes and not at my hands.

Now look. *so softly* Oh, look. I don't wear a bra to battle. It isn't lucky. A succubus won't wear a bra, either. So you can see almost all of my breasts. As I breathe … soft … and slow … *breathing* … you can watch my breasts push against my unzipped shirt. And my arms are caught in my jacket, behind me. … Captive. It would be so easy for you to finish baring me. Just a tug of your fingers, and my breasts would fall right out of my uniform … *whispers* free … and naked … and yours.

softly You're sitting so close to me now, I can feel your breath warm on my cheek.

aroused Soldier, I couldn't possibly get my hands loose from my jacket fast enough to stop you from taking hold of my breasts. *whispers* Do you want to hold my breasts? In your firm hands? Do my tits excite you? Does it excite you that you could strip me topless in a heartbeat?

teases Here, I'll help. If I just squirm and wriggle, like this, mmmm, with my arms captured behind me, *she makes soft little noises as she squirms* ahh! Look at that. My battle shirt slipped right off my nipples. You can see them. Look. My nipples are so swollen. They ache to be touched. Look how my breasts lift as I breathe. So … so … sofffft.

A succubus wants you to feel powerful, like you could just HAVE her, like you could TAKE her and RAVISH her, like she would just surrender in your arms and moan for you. *she moans softly whispers* I'm helpless. Are you going to touch my nipples?

quivery

gasps Ah!

I ... guess that's a yes!

Mmmmn. It's okay. You can do that. You can put your hands on my tits.

whispers Oh god.

so aroused You can cup them ... caress them ... mmmmn, squeeze them. *a whimper of need*

They're so soft in your hands.

quivery See? Mmm. I'm half naked and quivering in your arms. Oh, soldier, your hands on my tits, mmmn. *whispers* Under what's left of my uniform, my panties are soaked.

I'm helpless.

Except, if I was a succubus, I wouldn't actually be helpless. I'd be mere minutes from devouring your soul. *moans* Ohhhh, yes, yes, YES, do that. Mmm, do that. Tug at my nipples ... *whimpers* ... like that.

moaning softly

Oh, your hands feel so good.

Oh god, recruit! Kiss me.

Kiss me.

long, sensual kissing, and her soft little moans into the kiss

breathless

Oh, you've never been kissed like that?

Mmmm. That's how a succubus will kiss you, if she finds you unprepared on the plains of passion and fire tomorrow. Her small, soft tongue will tease and caress your tongue, like she's inviting you to take everything you want. To take ALL of her. To own her with a kiss.

sultry Own me, soldier. Kiss me again, and own me.

moaning, muffled, into his kiss

the sound of a zipper during the kiss

quivery I guess I can't really blame a succubus for wanting to capture you, soldier, when you kiss like that. When your hands feel like a god's on my tits. *moans* Here, let me reach down and …

giggles Oh, how you jumped! When I took your cock in my small, soft hands. *giggles* At least that blush has got some color back in your cheeks. Why so shy? It's okay, I won't hurt you. *giggles* Mmmm, I'm just going to pull your magnificent hard cock out. *breathes* Just for a moment. *moans* I only need a moment.

Mmm-hmmm, I wriggled my hands free and unzipped you while we kissed. All sneaky-like. *giggles* That's what a succubus does. *teases* Distracts you with pleasure so you don't even notice when she's taking more ... and more. Until it's much too late.

Mmm. I'll just trail small ... *kissing* ... sweet ... *kissing* ... wet kisses ... *kissing* ... along your neck ... *kissing*

... while my fingers caress your powerful cock. *kissing* My fingers are sooo soft. So gentle ... mmmmm. *whispers* And you're throbbing in my hands.

Mmmmm.

giggling Don't pull back... Why ARE you so shy?

gasps Wait ... you ... are you serious? You're a virgin?

whispers Oh, wow.

Wow.

Oh, soldier, you ARE unprepared to resist the wiles of a succubus.

Oh my god.

Okay, I better GET you ready, then. Virgins are REALLY vulnerable in battle. I can't BELIEVE they sent you. Oh my god. *nervous giggle*

Okay, here. Um. Listen. It's SO important that if you DO get captured by a succubus, that you DON'T cum in her. Not in her tight pussy, not in the warm grip of her ass, not in her soft, wet little mouth. You're still safe until she gets your semen ... and your soul. You CAN'T cum in her. Do you understand? You HAVE to be able to resist her.

What do you mean, 'how'? 'How do you resist...'? Oh my poor boy.

breathily All right, I'll show you. But while I do ...

whispers Don't. Cum.

Just don't.

Okay?

Okay, I'm going to keep ... playing ... with your hard virgin cock. Mmm, with my delicate, small hands. Like this. Mmmm. And YOU are going to practice enduring EVERYthing I do to you. Do you understand?

Good boy.

There, feel me stroking you slowly. You can handle it, can't you ... *giggles* ... while I handle you? Mmm. What if I ... caress your glans with my thumb ... just ... like ... this ...

Mmmmm, I can tell you like that.

aroused breathing

softly You love this, don't you? Having your fellow soldier stripped naked to the waist. As I devote myself to your pleasure. Do my hands feel good on your cock? Mmmm. Let me whisper in your ear.

whispers Tonight, don't think of me as your fellow soldier. Tonight, I'm your hot, high-breasted, aroused little slut. I'm your temptress, your harlot, with my soft hands and my wet, eager mouth ... *a wet, eager kiss giggles* Oh, how your cock hardens for me! Mmm. I like it. I really like how your cock feels. Hard as steel when I squeeze ... *soft little gasp* ... but your skin is soft as silk. Wow. You would feel SO good in my mouth.

But ... a succubus isn't just going to deepthroat you like a girl at a brothel on your homeworld, okay? She's going to tease you. She's going to want you to feel as adored, as worshipped, as powerful as a god. She'll caress you so, so gently with her fingers, like this. Then she might get on her knees ... like this ... here, by the fire ...

breathlessly ... I'm kneeling. With my face right here. Your cock warm against my cheek. A succubus might just tease the tip of your cock, just breathe across it, soft ... and warm ... like this ...

she breathes out slowly

Mmmm. How you twitch when I do that.

She might kiss ... *kissing*

And lick ... *licking*

... her way gently ...

kissing and licking

... down your shaft ...

licking

... to suckle at your balls, mmmmmm, sucking one at a time into her mouth, while her hand begins to work your cock, slow and sweet, like this ...

suckling sounds

Mmmm. Mmmm.

You smell SO good, soldier. *moans* So manly. Mmm, fuck. *suckling* Mmm. Mmm.

Everything else down here smells like sulphur … and brimstone. But you … oh god, you smell good.

suckling gently

Okay, any succubus you meet out there tomorrow would tease you a LOT longer, but … *breathless* … I really need your cock in my mouth right now. And YOU need the practice. So, here we go.

I'm going to lick the tip of your beautiful, virgin cock … *licking* … mmmmm … oh wow … I'll just close my lips around it gently and …

improv sweet, sensual blowjob sounds

mmmphhh mmm mmm mmmm, your cock feels amazing in my mouth!

mmm mmmm mmm

Feel me suck in my cheeks and just MMMMMMMMMMMM

blowjob noises

panting Do you like this? Do you like being in my mouth?

blowjob sounds

Mmm I need to tease your balls with my fingertips while I mmm mmmm mmmphh

improv a fast, passionate blowjob for a few moments

Mmmphh! Steady, soldier!

vigorous blowjob sounds

a muffled, surprised sound

gasps I can taste your precum. Salty and ... warm. Mmmmmmm. *whispers* Do not. Do NOT. Don't you DARE cum.

sucking wildly, moaning around his cock

suddenly she stops

Wait ... wait ... your cock is twitching, and your balls are tight. *panting* Oh, we have to stop, we have to stop.

You ... are getting SO hard. *a little moan of need*

Soldier, if you can't even resist MY charms, how will you survive a succubus? What if she knocks you out, and when you wake up, she has you tied up on the lava plain, and she is sucking your cock against your will while hot volcanoes erupt all around you? How will you keep YOUR volcano from erupting? And what if she decides to ride your cock like a hot, tight slut? What will you do then? Will you be able to resist while her snug little cunt milks your cock dry?

breathless Well, let's practice ... and find out.

rustling clothes

What am I doing? What does it look like I'm doing, soldier? I'm taking off the rest of my uniform.

And ... shimmying out of my panties. *an aroused little sigh* Sliding them down my hips ... my thighs ... my smooth, long legs ... baring my soft, naked little cunt ... Ohhh, the night air feels so good against my wet sex.

breathes the word Yes.

Now, turn around. Let me see your hands. Mmm-hmmm. Good boy. I'll just take these wet panties and ... tie your wrists with them! *giggles* There we go. Mmm-hmm, just like that, *softly, sweetly* just like that. There, um, try to tug free for a moment. I twisted my panties around pretty tight, but they ARE just lace panties, I need to make sure they can hold you. Okay, good, yes. MMMMM, yes. Squirm like that. *aroused* Just like that. Oh, wow, you have a ... really enticing body, soldier. And a very, very hard cock. *a whimper of need* Oh, the way it throbs. I bet if I so much as look at your cock, you will burst and cum all over my hands and my tits.

a lustful moan

Oh, we can't have that. *reluctantly* We can't.

catching her breath Okay, now, as a succubus, I'd thrust you down on your back, like this. Mmm-hmm. You're not going ANYwhere, soldier. I have you tied up with my own panties, right here by my watch-fire, and I'm kneeling over you, warm and wet, and you're going to practice RESISTING me.

aroused I guess you haven't seen a cunt before, have you? Look. *whispers* Look.

My pussy is soft … and warm … and if I spread my folds with my fingers, mmmmm … open.

I'm open for you.

And so … tight.

Mmm. Don't be shy. See? My warm sex is just like a small, soft blossom. Like a flower. Nothing to be scared of. Well *giggles* unless it's a succubus's pussy. Then that sweet flower will EAT YOUR SOUL.

soft, aroused breathing Oh, but this flower … this pussy … my wet tight sex, right here, she just wants to kiss and caress your cock and make you feel so, so good. Personally, I think I have the best pussy in the regiment. *moans* In fact, I'm sure of it.

Look, I'll slide one of my fingers inside me.

moans

See how my pussy grips my finger?

a shuddering moan See how wet … and soft?

Just think about how good I'm going to feel around your cock. *whispers* I'm going to feel so good.

Here, I'll straddle you. Press myself to you … hot … and wet. *moans* Oh fuck, your cock feels really, REALLY good pressed against my naked, wet little pussy. *moans* Oh, wow.

Oh, wow. OH, you feel so GOOD just rubbing against my folds like that! *whimpers of need*

Here, feel my soft fingers curl around your cock. Oh YES.

Yes, you beautiful virgin, I AM going to put your cock inside me. How ELSE are you going to learn to resist cumming inside a succubus? You are in SO MUCH danger, recruit. I can't just send you out there with this hard, amazing cock that has NEVER been touched, that could spasm at the first warm grip of a woman's cunt. You have GOT to be prepared!

And besides, *giggles* it will take the edge off for me, too. I'm all KINDS of keyed up, waiting all night for a battle where anything might happen to me, where I might get captured and gangraped by incubi, or strapped down tight and eaten out until I just DIE of orgasms. I wouldn't mind being better prepared myself.

Here.

I'm going to let my tight, wet entrance just … kiss the tip of your cock. Mmm-hmm. The gentlest kiss, like a virgin girl might give you at a dance. *sultry* But I am no virgin. And we are not going to DANCE, soldier. We are going to FUCK.

sultry and commanding Now give me that cock.

I'll just slide you inside me and … *she cries out as his cock fills her*

gasping Oh, yes! YES, you're big. Fuck! And I'm so slick around your cock!

moaning I'm just going to rock my hips and ... FUCKKKK!!!

she muffles her moaning with her hand, for a few moments, just riding him hard and moaning into her hand

gaspy Okay, oh GOD, if I scream like a succubus in heat, it won't matter that we're the only sentries this side of the ridge. The entire camp, over there, WILL hear you fuck me.

sultry Oh, I don't care. Fuck me.

Fuck me, soldier.

But. Don't. Cum.

moans, in heat

What's that? *moans* You think no succubus could possibly ride your cock as good as this? Oh god. *moans* When you say things like THAT to a girl ... mmmm ... *flattered and wild with lust* ohhh, you are going to get SUCH a ride now, soldier. I'm going to dig my nails into your chest and just RIDE you like a stallion. Fuck YES. I need you deep in me. *whimpers* Deeper. Deeper! *whimpering as she tries to hold back her moans, passionate and hot, as she RIDES him*

Fuck. You feel so good. And I'm so tight. *moans* It's been too long since my own training. Oh, yes, you good GOOD boy, you take that cunt. You TAKE THAT CUNT. Fucking TAKE me. Feel me squeeze down on your cock! *cries out in lust and joy* Yes. Yes! Yes!

You are doing SO. GOOD. Now make it last. Be a good boy for me. Please please please be a good boy and don't cum. Don't cum. Don't cum.

cries out Yes! Grab my breasts! Oh YES, soldier, squeeze my tits. Oh, fucking SQUEEZE them! *squeals in pleasure* I'm so WET! Oh, what you DO to me!

wild moans

No, don't you DARE cum, soldier! You can DO this! *panting* You can hold it! You can! You can resist a succubus, soldier! You can do this!

moans

Oh yes, you buck those hips! You whimper and moan for me, soldier!

You didn't know a woman could do this to you, did you? You had no idea how powerful a woman can be when she's riding your cock. What if I swirl my hips like this? *moans* How about that? *panting* You like that? You like that?

So you think I fuck as good as a succubus, is that right? Is that what you think? I could be one, you know. I could be one of those hellgirl seductresses who've infiltrated your camp. I could be here to thin your numbers before tomorrow's battle. *sultry, teasing* I could be taking your soul right now, just pretending to be a sweet, friendly soldier-girl who wants to help train you. How would you know?

But … as long as you don't cum in me, it doesn't matter, right? You'll never need to know whether I'm your wet, soaked little army-slut … or a predator here to EAT you.

You don't need to KNOW, you just need to FUCK.

So take my hips in your hands and fuck me, soldier! Fuck me!

moaning Yes! Yes! Yes!

her voice goes low and animal-intense with heat If I were a succubus, I would grip your hair right now, just like this, right now while your amazing cock fucks me silly, and I'd force your head back, my mouth hot on your neck, like this, *moans* and I'd tell you to CUM.

fiercely You know you want to. You want to flood my pussy!

DO IT!

she squeals!! Cum in me, soldier, PLEASE!

Fuck me full of cum!

Fuck! Fuck! FUCK! I'm going to cum! I'm going to cum! I'm going to CUM! Feel me squeeze and ripple around your cock, feel my hand in your hair as I RIDE you! Fill me, soldier, fill me! You CUM FOR ME LIKE A GOOD BOY!

YOU CUM IN MY PUSSY RIGHT NOW, SOLDIER!

CUM! CUM! CUM IN ME! CUM WITH ME! CUM IN ME! CUM INSIDE ME! GIVE ME YOUR CUM! GIVE ME YOUR SOUL! GIVE IT TO ME! CUM INSIDE ME! YES, YES, PULSE IN ME, DO IT TO ME, OH GOD THAT'S SO HOT, OH GOD THAT'S SO HOT, OH HOLY HELL YES YES YES YES YES!

her squeals of orgasm

panting after

breathing hard Oh soldier.

Oh you good boy.

shaky Ohh, ohh, that was … that was amazing. Oh, you are the BEST fuck. *giggles* Oh unholy FUCK. My thighs are shaking.

giggles You were sooo good.

Your cum is going to be leaking down my leg all night.

whispers hotly I get to go to battle tomorrow on the plains of fire and lust with some of your cum sticky on my thigh, and with some of your hot, sticky cum still inside my pussy.

moans

Mmm, yes, put your arms around me. Mmm. Oh, you are SUCH a good fuck. Are you sure you were a virgin? Holy HELL.

soft little whimpers of pleasure

Yes, I know I'm clenching around your cock in little aftershocks of pleasure. I can't help it. You are a fucking GOD. How you fucked me. Mmmm.

My … good … boy.

Shhh. Here, I'll press my breasts to your chest and just lie here on top of you. So sweaty. And so good. *whispers* Yes, put your hands on me.

Mmmn.

Can you feel my heartbeat beneath my breast? My heart is racing. For you.

a long, passionate kiss, with her soft little sounds as she kisses him

Mmmm, hold me. Do you think we woke the camp? *teasing* Do you think the other new recruits are jealous, tossing on their cots while they listened to my screams of pleasure in the night, just over the ridge, just out of their reach? Mmmm, but not out of YOUR reach. You've got me. *giggles* Mmm, and I've got YOU.

whispers I'm a pretty good fuck too, aren't I? *moans* I am an amazing fuck.

Do you see the volcanoes erupting out there in the dark, spurting all their lust and fire into the night sky? *giggles* I bet when I gripped your cock, I made them all orgasm too. See? Whoosh! *giggles* Even the Dark Queen herself can't outdo THAT.

giggling

Just lie here with me … and inside me, soldier. And in a minute or two, you get to find out whether you still have your soul. Because you totally FAILED that lesson, you know. *giggles* You DID pump me full of your cum.

Oh, you were just following my orders? Is that so?

amused What world do you think this is, Earth? You're not supposed to follow orders! You're supposed to be a rebel storming the gates of hell! You're supposed to RESIST!

giggles

So. *teasing* Now you get to find out if I'm still your eager little slut in uniform … or. A succubus. A lustful, dangerous, HUNGRY succubus. Who thinks your soul is as tasty as your hard cock.

Which one do YOU think I am?

giggles

You'll see.

Kiss me, silly boy.

passionate kissing, and her moans into the kiss

whispers Either way, I can tell you one thing.

You …

are mine.

kissing

the scene ends

5

A Sultry Elfgirl Paladin Teaches You How to Kiss Her, Titfuck Her, and Cum in Her Mouth

TAGS: [F4M] [Sensual] [Nurturing] [Virgin Listener] [Kissing] [Titjob] [Blowjob] [Cock Worship] [Enthusiastic Throatfuck] [Adoration] [I'll Keep Your Cock so Warm and Safe] [Make Me Sticky with Your Cum] [Good Boy]

ambient nighttime forest sounds, and we hear the buckles and rustling as the elfgirl undresses

gently What am I doing? I'm taking my armor off, of course. It is the full moon, and it is time to oil my body by moonlight. To lie back on the forest moss and bathe in moonlight, to let my smooth skin drink the moon's magic, is very important to an elfgirl. Don't worry, my chieftain. I am keeping my sword close. There is always a risk of goblin raiders in these woods. Of course, after how I trounced them at Drata's Ford, they'd probably take one look at my sleek, pointed elven ears and run for their lives. *giggles* But don't worry. *giggles* I will fight and slay them naked if I have to.

I promised your betrothed I would deliver you to her village safely, and I am Vanna the paladin; I keep my promises. I am the most skilled paladin from the elven cities, from the gleaming towers of the dawn. My hair is gold, my breasts full and perfect. I am brave in battle and in bed. In combat, my blade catches the sun. In love, I ride my companion until he gives more seed than he ever knew he could. I am a paladin and pure, and hot with life. When your intended asked our people for an escort for you, they chose well. I will let no harm befall you.

the sound of her getting oil on her hands

Mmm. It's warm, scented oil. For my breasts. For my sleek thighs and legs. Mmmmm.

moaning softly as she rubs the oil into her body

after a moment, she giggles You're blushing. Do human women not bathe in moonlight in the sight of their men? Hmm. That's too bad. I am told a woman oiled and bathing in the moon is a good sight. That it hardens a man and sharpens his senses. That when a male watches a woman performing the moon ritual, it makes him better. In council. And in bed.

It's all right. You may watch.

I don't mind.

soft sighs and moans as she oils her body

a soft gasp Oh, these nipples. Unnh, they're so hard. Though the night is hot.

It's been too long, I think, since I had an elflord hard … and mighty … inside me.

I must … I must do something about that when I return to my own country.

How your face burns, mortal chieftain. Surely you've seen a woman naked before?

surprised You … you haven't?

But … you're a chieftain! Surely you've had a woman warrior of your own people strip away her armor and throw herself to your furs and open her legs to harden her chieftain before a council, or to heat her body before combat?

You … you have no women warriors?

Well.

That's silly.

Surely you don't rely on men to do the fighting? *amused and even a little delighted* Such irrational, hot-tempered tornadoes of testosterone and fury. Men are good for councils and bed, not battle. Every woman knows that.

You mortals will never stop surprising me.

she moans softly, and we hear the wet sounds of the oil

Ooooh, this oil. Mmm. My hands are so soft. I better part my legs … opening like a blossom. Mmmm. The day's riding chafes my thighs. I will oil them until they glisten, wet, in the night. Mmm.

softly An elfgirl should never face her enemies with dry skin or a dry flower between her thighs. It's bad luck. And who knows what dangers the night hours will bring? Ogres or goblins or wolfmen with howling in their heart. I will face your enemies with my body hot and wet and alive, with all the thunder of my heart, and I will protect you.

You've … never seen a woman's flower?

giggles You're teasing me, you must be. You're … you're not serious?! Never?

tenderly Here, look.

Mmm. This is what we look like.

Well, this is what I look like. Every woman's flower is different and lovely in her own way. Mmm-hmm, this golden down is soft and … sweet … between my thighs. My petals are swollen and ready for pleasure. Ohhh. Oooooh, my fingers feel good there, dripping with oil.

Mmm.

aroused and curious If you've never seen a woman's flower, does that mean … you've never seen your betrothed's?

Oh? You're mating with her to forge peace between your peoples? Not for love? Well, I hope she proves loving and lovely to you nonetheless.

Oh, she's a widow? Oh, I see. I see why you look so frightened. She knows the ways of battle and of bed, and you are a virgin. You're frightened you won't please her, or that you'll freeze when you see her, even with your cock hard in your fist, the way a warrior trembles when her first goblin raid rushes screaming at her from the woods?

softly Oh, you poor boy. You must be terrified.

I see the ways of your people have not prepared you well. Sweet boy. *so tenderly* How may I help?

You may ask me anything. It is a sacred night. I am soft and naked by moonlight, oiling my wet flower and my thighs, and it is the ninth moon, a holy night for the elves. And I am commanded to bring you safe and strong to your new life.

How may I help you be strong and brave, beautiful chieftain?

Oh? You think it might help if you … if you know how to touch a woman, before you come to this widow's bed?

Hmm.

Well, come sit by me, gentle human. Help me oil my legs, and let's talk.

Here, hold out your hands. I will lift this ewer of sacred oil and pour …

we hear her pouring oil into his hands

There you go.

Put it on me.

Mmmm, yes, oh. Caress my legs. Rub the oil warm and sweet into my skin. Mmmm. That feels so good. Your hands feel good on me.

Mmm. What have you done so far, mortal? *she listens* ... You haven't ... kissed a girl? I see.

so, so gentle Would you like to?

Would you like to kiss me, while you rub oil into my body with your strong hands?

Here are my lips. They're soft ... and full ... and gentle. Would you like to kiss them?

Here, let me touch your cheek. My hand is warm from the oil. Shhh. Let me. I'll hold your face so gently and ... *whispers* here.

a sweet, warm kiss

whispers Yes.

That was a kiss.

softly breathing for a moment

But ... you'll need to open your mouth for this next part. Mmm-hmmm. Here. Just part your lips. There. *so softly* I'll teach you.

a gentle, sensual, open-mouthed kiss

a soft, sweet sigh after the kiss

Oh, you have a very lovely mouth. A woman could really enjoy kissing you.

kissing Mmm.

Here, I'll take your hand, bring your hand to my hair. I want you … to slide your fingers into my hair and just hold me while we kiss. *softly* Hold me like you want me.

so, so gently Do you want me?

whispers Show me how much. As you kiss me.

another kiss, more passionate

whispers You good boy.

softly Do you like how my mouth opens for you? How my tongue caresses yours? So warm and wet … welcoming your tongue into my mouth? *whispers* Welcoming you inside me?

a brief, open-mouthed, hungry kiss Mmmm.

Now, take a firmer grip. I don't know what your human women are like, but when you're with an elfgirl who has battled monsters and conquered warriors, when you kiss her, it's your chance to conquer HER. To overwhelm her with your hunger, your passion, your need. There's passion in you, mortal. I look in your eyes and see such … fire. Be brave. Kiss me.

a hot kiss

after a moment, she moans into his mouth, surprised

breathless Oh! Yes. Like that. Take hold of me like that. Oh, do that again. Kiss m-Mmmphh!

kissing, moaning into his mouth

panting softly That's it. Now the next thing you should – mmmphhhh!

he kisses her more roughly

she moans passionately

giggles Okay, yes. You're getting the idea. Mmmm.

kissing

Now bite my lip. Take a fistful of my hair and bite my lip and kiss me until I can't breathe. My body will squirm for you if you do that. Let my body know you're going to overcome me here on the forest moss. Kiss me like that, mortal. Kiss me like that.

a long, fierce kiss, and her squeal muffled by his mouth when he bites her

panting Now I'm flushed, too. Put your hands on my breasts, mortal. My breasts are full and voluptuous and so … soffft … and they need your hands. And more oil.

she moans sweetly

Oh, you have strong hands. Such strong, human hands. I quiver for you in the moonlight. Mmmm, grip my breasts. Squeeze my breasts. Oh, mortal. Yes. Oil me. Rub warm oil into my tits.

I can hardly breathe. *sultry* Don't let me breathe. Kiss me again.

hot, passionate kisses

gasps Yes, my neck. Like that. Oh yes. The throat is a warrior's most vulnerable place. And I am naked without armor. Ah! Yes, bite the skin on my neck. Oh! Oh! *panting* If your widow bride is anything like an elfgirl, she'll want to be marked the morning after you mate. She'll want to see the bruises of your passion on her body, from your mouth, your teeth, from the press of your fingertips gripping her as you give her love. Squeeze my breasts hard, mortal, and kiss my neck.

Mmmm.

moaning

panting softly Good boy. Good boy.

Give me your hand. Here, here, let me … put your hand between my thighs. Ohhhh. Between my soft thighs. Here, right here, feel. Feel what your kisses do to me. Feel what you DO to a woman. *moans* Feel how hot and wet and slick my petals are? That's not the oil, mortal. That's my own nectar, that's my warm elven honey. I am dripping at your touch.

breathes the words Touch me.

Yes, like that. Ahh, ahh! Gentle and slow. Oh, oh. You can bite my mouth and my neck, but you need to be gentle down here. At first. *sultry* I might not mind if you bite me there later, beautiful human boy. Just a little bite. Ohh, ohhh …

but I'm an elfgirl, I'm not as fragile as your human girls might be. Be gentle with THEM, mortal. At least at first. Ohhh, yes. *whispers* Does my softness feel good to you? Here … I'll guide your fingers. Right here. This, this little flowerbud just above my blossom, this, *whispers* you need to touch this. *whimpering with need* Touch this, my chieftain. Touch me here.

moaning

Yes, slow teasing circles, just like that. Just like that. Here, here. *panting* Run your fingertips between my folds, get some of my honey on them, and draw my warm honey up over my flowerbud. Mmmmm, YES, like that. Ohhhh, that's how you oil THIS part of my body, mortal. Ohh. Ohhh. Ohhh.

Now kiss me. Kiss … and lick … and nibble … at my neck, my shoulders, my breasts, my body … wherever you want to. Do what feels natural. Don't think … just … caress me, EXPLORE me with your mouth. Let my moans at your touch excite you and encourage you. And explore my body. My body is naked and oiled and hot in the moonlight, and it's yours to explore and enjoy. Enjoy me, mortal.

moaning Oh yes, oh yes.

Ohh … ohhh … you like licking circles around my nipples, don't you? You like how I quiver. Oh good boy, good boy … mmm … ohhh! Your breath warm across my nipple. Mmm!

giggles How you tease.

I like it.

I really, really like it.

Mmmm. Have ... have you seen how babies suckle? Lovers do that too. You can do that. I don't ... I don't have ... any milk ... for you to drink ... but you can still suckle at my full, warm breasts. Go ahead. Suckle me, mortal. While you caress me between my thighs.

improv her breathless moans as he does

Ohh yes. Oh yes. Beautiful human. Oh! Oh! I'll tell you a secret. A woman's nipples are so, so sensitive!!! Especially an elfgirl's! I'll weave my fingers into your hair and hold your head to my breasts. Mmm. Mmm.

Ohhh, I'm so wet! My warm elven honey is flooding your fingertips! Mmmn!

Here, get your cock out. Shh, it's okay. It's okay. Whether your cock is large or small, or thin or thick, it will feel so warm inside a woman. And she'll hold you so tightly. Gently and sweetly inside her. And you'll excite a woman with your whole body. Your cock, your fingers, your hands, your mouth, your breath across her skin, *moans* the roll of your hips. Even the groans and grunts from your lips will excite her. *moans* You excite ME. Please, let me see your cock. Please.

so softly I'll help.

we hear the sounds of her opening his garments to free his cock

Ahhh. That ... is a good cock. Your cock is so beautiful. It's just right for me. *whispers* Just right.

Here, I'll take your cock in my oiled hands. Oooh, oooh, I love how you feel. Like a blade of hard steel sheathed inside skin that's so soft, so soft.

whispers I want this cock between my breasts.

comforting Shh-shh. I'm going to get your cock so hard and so ready. I'm going to take such good care of this cock. Be brave, my beautiful boy.

breathless Here, my chieftain. I'll show you … I'll show you what a gentle, warm, woman can do with your cock.

Mmm. I'll slide down like this … ohhh … here, yes, put your cock right here, between my breasts. Mmm-hmm. I'll hold them and press them around your hard cock. That way your hands are free. Mmmn, you can keep reaching back and teasing me. *moans* With your fingers. Oh. You can … you can put a finger inside me while we do this, if you want to. The night-blossom between my thighs is soft … and yielding … and so open. I'm open for you. Feel my opening kiss your fingertip. *moans* So soft. *moans*

whispers I'm so soft and so good.

Put it inside me. My beautiful, brave chieftain. Slide your finger inside me.

Yes, oooh! Gentle! mmm. Like that. *breathless* Like that. Ohhh! I love your finger inside me! Oh, I love it.

we hear the slick sounds of her oiled breasts around his cock, the wet sounds of her pussy around his finger

I'll squeeze your cock so gently between my breasts. Here, just rock your hips. Thrust. Yes. Thrust. Ohhh. Let me take care of you. I'm going to take care of everything. Just roll your hips and thrust that cock back … and forth … back and forth … between my hot, oiled breasts. Oh, mortal boy. Look at my eyes, soft and shining in the moonlight. Watch my tits, slick and glistening and so warm around your cock.

she grunts sweetly as he fucks her breasts

seductive You can go faster if you want to. I can take it.

soft, feminine gasps and grunts intensify

so aroused I can smell your musk. Your masculine, human musk … *trembles* … it does things to me. I love how you smell. Oh, oh, yes, ride me, beautiful boy. Ride me hard and fuck my hot elven tits. Fuck my tits! Unnh! Unnh!

Ohh. I need a hand free. Here, my chieftain, you've one hand on my elven flower. Put the other hand on my left tit, help me hold my tits for you. That's it. Oh, your hand feels good on my breast! I'm going to reach and … mmm … grip your ass. Oh, feel my nails. This. THIS grip on your ass means I want you. That a woman WANTS you. A woman wants your cock between her tits, in her mouth. In her soft elven pussy. Ah! That's what it means when a woman squeezes your ass like this! Mmm.

Now, there's soft skin just behind your balls, the perineum, I'm going to caress it with my fingertips. Mmm-hmmm. Just like this. *softly* Just like this. Ohhhh! *giggles* You like this. Yes. Do my fingers excite you? Does your hot, naked paladin excite you? I can feel your excitement and desire in the surge of your hips. Yes, yes! Fuck my tits! Fuck my tits!

wild moans

a sudden cry Oh! A second finger inside me! Ah! Yes, mortal, YES! You can do that! Oh! I'm so tight, I'm so tight, your fingers are so big in me! Here, mortal, curl your fingertips, curl them like … like you're beckoning me to come to you. Oh yes, mortal, like that, like that, I'll come to you, I'll cum to you, I'll cum to you! Mortal, mortal, mortal! Oh goddess! This feels so good! Your cock feels so good beween my breasts! So thick! I'm holding your cock so warm and so safe between my tits! *almost sobbing with sheer need* Oh mortal! Oh mortal! Feel me caress and massage the skin behind your balls, yes, yes, oh, fuck my tits, fuck my tits, fuck my tits, make my tits BOUNCE for you, human! I'm going to…. I'm going to … I'm going to OH MY GODDESS I'm going to … oh mortal, are you? Are you? Yes, I feel you pulsing between my tits! Yes! Yes! You can cum on my tits, mortal! You can cum on my tits! Cum between my tits! You're safe between my tits! I'm holding your cock so safe and hot, you beautiful, beautiful boy!!! Cover my tits in your cum! Pleae cum on me, my good boy! Please! Cum on my tits! Cum on my tits! Cum on my tits! Cum, cum –

her scream of orgasm

sweet little sounds afterward

Mmmm. Did you feel me tighten around your fingers? *whispers* I've soaked your fingers in my juices, beautiful boy.

Mmmm.

Oh, your cum is all over the tops of my tits. My neck. My shoulders. So hot and sticky.

softly Gaze down at me, mortal. At Vanna the paladin. My voluptuous tits and my neck sticky with your cum. My eyes are soft and adoring.

grateful You gave me your cum.

so softly Feel me run my nails gently, teasingly along your thighs. Oh, mortal. A woman will feel so good when you give her your cum.

Mmm-hmm. You see. Nothing to be afraid of. You will be so brave in bed, mortal. *whispers* You were so brave and so hard, cumming between my tits.

Mmm. Feel me tease … your shaft … with my fingers. Your cock is so sticky. *giggles* Here, let me lick … and suck … it clean. Don't worry. My mouth will be so warm and soft and welcoming. I promise.

slow licking

whispers I like how you twitch against my tongue. Mmm. And your cum tastes … *licking* … salty. Like the sea.

licking

I want more.

whispers I want you in my mouth.

I want to let you cum in my mouth.

Shh-shhh. I've got you, beautiful boy. I'm going to hold your cock so safe in my mouth, and I'm going to show you how to cum down an elfgirl's throat by moonlight.

softly I'm going to swallow your cum. Every drop of your hot cum. I want to swallow for you, lovely human.

Here, let me just … breathe … across the tip of your cock.

a slow, gentle exhale

whispers Your cock excites me.

another exhale

My fingers caressing your balls. So gently.

another exhale

Mmmm. I'll kiss your tip.

slow, slow, seductive kissing at the head of his cock

Mmm, your cock is so beautiful and so good. It's just right for me. *whispers* Oh, your cock is so right for me.

Let me run my tongue from the base of your shaft alllllll the way up to the tip. Slowwwly. Just loving your cock with my warm, wet tongue.

she does that, slow and sensual

Mmmm. This cock. I want to do that again, beautiful human. I want to love this cock with my soft eleven tongue, by moonlight Here, hold my breasts for me, keep them warm in your hands, and I'll press my soaked little elven flower against your hip ... mmmm ... like that ... feel me so wet and slick ... while I love this cock with my lips ... *kissing* ... and my tongue ...

licking for a while

breathless Now ...

... I'm going to put you in my mouth.

improv a slow, sensual, loving blowjob, moaning softly around his cock

breathless after a few moments Does my mouth feel good on your cock? My chieftain, look at my mouth on your cock. At my eyes gazing up at you as I suck your cock.

sucking

Your hot ...

kissing the tip

Human ...

kissing the tip

emphasizing the word seductively ... cock.

she takes him in her mouth suddenly again, a deeper, passionate blowjob

Mmm, I love the warm weight of your cock on my tongue. Oh, human.

sucking

suddenly Mmmphh! MMPHH! MMMPHHH!

panting, gasping for air Ah, your hand on my head! *panting* You can do that. *sultry* Yes, you can do that, mortal. You can push me down on your cock.

rougher blowjob noises

panting

giggles Good boy. But every woman's different. *teasing* She may not be able to tell you with her mouth full whether she enjoys that or not. So you'll have to pay attention like a good boy and listen to how she moans around your cock. Mmmm, I like it though. I've fought ogres and goblins and dragonkind. I'm not afraid of a hard, thick cock. Fuck my mouth, beautiful mortal.

he shoves her down on his cock

improv a throatfuck and her muffled moans and sounds

gulping for air Yes, yes, press my nose to your groin, your balls to my chin, and fuck my throat, you gorgeous boy! As much as you need to. Pull my hair, ahhh! Grab my slender, pointed ears if you need to, anything you need, just fuck this voluptuous elfgirl's throat! Uurrrk urrrg uurrrg

throatfucking sounds

panting That's a good boy. So much more confident now. Are my moans around your cock helping? Fuck my throat, mortal. Fuck my throat. I'll moan for you! Put your cock deep in my mou-Mmmph urrgr urrrrg

throatfucking sounds

desperate with arousal Cum down my throat, mortal! I need it, I need it, I need your cum! Urrrg urrg urrrg AHHHH! Cum down my throat! Cum down my throat!

hot throatfucking sounds

then the sound of her being held down on his cock, breathless, just making helpless little sounds as she flexes her throat

several slow swallows, gulps

a whimper

then she is off his cock and gulping down breaths of air

after a moment, she laughs breathlessly

Oh, you beautiful boy. Beautiful human! Oh my goddess.

giggling helplessly, barely with enough breath to

I guess I know I excited you, then. Mmmm. Did you like throatfucking Vanna the elfgirl? Did you like cumming down my throat?

giggles

Whoo! I needed that! *giggles* I'm slick with sweat. Wow. Here, mmm, take me in your arms.

kissing him

I'll hold your face in my hands.

soft, sweet noises

I'm so grateful for what you gave me tonight, beautiful virgin boy. I want to kiss your neck.

kissing

…and your chin.

giggles

kissing

Your cheeks.

kissing

Ohhh. Your beautiful, beautiful eyelids.

kissing

Mmmm. Beautiful, boy.

kissing

whispers You fucked my throat.

And my tits.

I'm sticky with your cum, my chieftain. I may go to battle tomorrow with your cum dried and sticky on me, beneath my armor.

kissing

Feel me trace my fingers down your chest. *whispers* I just want to hold this cock in my small … soft … fingers … ahhh, like this, mmm, while you hold me naked in the moonlight.

We'll keep each other warm.

Mmm. Mortal. Remember, be gentle with your widow bride at first. Not every girl likes to have her face held down on a hard, thick human cock. *giggles* For all I know, human girls are dainty little things. Don't break her. *giggles* But … if … if you happen to have your cock in her mouth and she is moaning like she's on FIRE, then be brave, human boy. Just watch her eyes … and guide her with your powerful hands … and let her love on your cock.

Mmm. Mmm, this cock.

whispers You human men and your cocks.

I really love your cock.

Oh … you think I'm hot, too?

giggles I'm glad. Mmmn. *teasing* It's hardly surprising, though. I'm elven. We elfgirls are sensual … and wet … and a dream of pleasure.

Oh? You'd still choose me out of a battalion of naked, oiled elven women? *sultry* Really?

she coos, aroused and happy That's so sweet. Lovely human. *low and sultry* I'm REALLY going to love on this cock now. *giggles*

Kiss my mouth.

kissing him

she moans into his mouth

Mmmm. You are a good kisser, my chieftain. You really, really kiss me well.

passionate kissing

Rest a while and kiss me, mortal, while I play gently with this cock.

Adoringly Just kiss me.

kissing

… and touch my breasts. Ahhhh.

kissing and moaning

Your cock has fought a brave battle. And when it recovers, I'll guide this beautiful cock inside me. Inside my wet, tight body. *whispers* I'll put your cock in me.

I will squeeze … and grip … and milk your cock … *whispers* … with my tight elven pussy.

Mmm. I'll teach you how to hold a woman's body while she rides you in bed. Oh, mortal, I will teach you so much. I'll make sure you're ready when we reach the village. Your widow bride will be so pleased and her soft human pussy will gush with love for you at what you do to her, I promise. You are so brave and so good, and I will teach you everything.

gentle kiss

whispers Everything.

Your cock will be inside me tonight. My wet heat will caress … and love … your cock.

kissing him hotly

I love holding you, and being held. Beautiful human, you're so safe and so good in my arms, my tits pressed to your chest. Mmm. I'm warm and feminine and so sticky with your cum on my tits. Mmm. Just hold me and kiss me while our bodies bathe in the moonlight. *breathless* Until you're ready to fuck me.

whispers Because I want you to fuck me. I want you in me so much.

My good boy. My beautiful boy. *breathless* Beautiful boy.

kissing

so tenderly Beautiful boy.

gentle kissing and soft little sighs and sounds from her, and gentle forest noises

Beautiful boy.

the scene ends

6

The Gunslinger Captured: Promise to Let Me Go, Bounty Hunter, And You Can Ravish Me

TAGS: [F4M] [Seduction] [Bondage] [Wild West] [Bosoms] [Nonconsent] [Blowjob] [Gunplay] Some [Fearplay] [Anal] [Deflowering] [Double Penetration] [Very Rough] [Creampie]

giggles Oh, look at you tipping your hat to me, Mister. Thank you kindly. But do tell me why you're barring my way down the stair to the main floor of this saloon? A gentleman steps aside and lets a lady by. And really with this flowing skirt and the petticoats under, I need the whole stair, Mister. I can't just wriggle by you like a fish midstream.

teasing Will you step aside, Mister, and let a lady by?

What's that? This stair is so narrow and treacherous-like that you'd be a right fool to let a woman walk down it all by herself? Well now. Aren't you a gentleman. And *gasps* your arm around my waist. You ARE forward, Mister. I begin to suspect you might not be any kind of a gentleman but more than half a ruffian. Pulling me close like this. What if I screamed?

her voice lowers Oh? You have ways of keeping a woman quiet? Is that so?

Your hands are getting mighty friendly, Mister. *softly* I think you should let me go before something untoward happens.

rustling garments

breathless little noises from her

softly I really am going to scream, Mister.

he shuts her up with a kiss

she makes sweet feminine noises into the kiss but does not scream

after the kiss, she is more breathless

Now isn't that a wonder. I didn't scream at all. I wonder why that is. I should have. I should have screamed like the saloon is on fire, with how you're manhandling me, Mister.

kissing

Mmm. I declare. You DO know how to kiss.

… Oh? You're inviting me upstairs? For a conversation and another kiss? Now what kind of a lady would I be if I said yes?

a laugh A happy lady? Is that so, Mister?

kissing

Well.

kissing

All right. You better escort me upstairs and show me a little more clearly what you mean, Mister. Otherwise I'll be lying in my bed all night and half the morning wondering just what you had in mind.

Optional sound effect: Their footsteps on the stair

sounds of passionate kissing, rustling clothes

breathless, hushed Are you trying to get into my bodice, Mister? We aren't even in your room yet. *kissing* Patience is a gentlemanly virtue … *kissing*

teasing But I see you are definitely no kind of gentleman.

kissing … a soft sound of arousal muffled under the kiss

hushed There. You get me through that door and in private, and you can have your wicked pleasure in me, Mister.

kissing

the sound of a door creaking open, then shutting

her soft, sweet moan into the kiss

the kissing interrupted by the click of a gun being cocked as she pulls her revolver on him

breathless There now. I'll just step back so I can keep you in my sights. No, don't you move a muscle, Mister. You just hold right there against that door, or my Smith and Wesson is going to give you a kiss will stay in your memory longer than my lips will. Good boy. That's it. Keep those hands out where I can see them proper in the moonlight from that window. That's right.

You got me quite disheveled, Mister, with your devilish kissing and your sweet talking and your hands on my bosom. Now you stay right there while I hold this gun in my left hand and button up my bodice with my right, and we'll have us a talk.

Tell me, why you were following me today? Did you think I wouldn't notice you slinking after me through the town like a serpent after a little mouse? I declare, you could scare a girl doing that. That ain't no kind of thing to do to a lady.

angrily, indignant at something he says Oh how dare you! I AM a lady, I am. No one's ever gotten beneath these petticoats yet, and you sure ain't fixing to.

… Yes, that's right, I did kill seven men in three states. And every one of them had it coming. You men think you own the world. Think you can have any woman you want, willing or no. Well I keep my Smith and Wesson gartered to my thigh, and my single-action revolver, she says I own myself and anyone says different is going to eat lead. Now just why ARE you following me? Be truthful with me, Mister. I never laid eyes on you before. What do you want with me?

Ha. Yes, I see your eyes on my bosom. I'm sure it's heaving prettily right now on account of how excited I am to shoot you dead in a minute. I'd have my dress buttoned up proper, only it seems you tore it. You men are such animals.

Now what do you really want?

A ... a bounty? *startled* You mean to tell me there's a bounty out on me?

squeaks How much?

That...that much?

breathless, awed I declare.

I've half a mind to turn mySELF in for that much.

Eighty dollars? Lord above. Who put eighty dollars on me? Who wants me that bad?

... The mayor of Houston? What?

His son! You mean to tell me that loudmouth groping drunkard I shot between the eyes was a mayor's son? I'm in a heap of trouble, aren't I?

But then so are you. You ain't getting no bounty on me, that's for sure. Now turn around and face the door and you just start praying that I have mercy in my heart I tie you up and leave you still breathing God's clean air while I get away. That's it ...

suddenly she gives a startled little gasp, and we hear her gun clatter to the floor

Why, you!!! *squirming* You had a henchman hiding, waiting to grab me, Mister? I declare, you are no kind of a gentleman! *struggling, grunting* You have your man get his filthy hands off me RIGHT now, or I swear I will scream fit to wake every lawman for miles. Let go of m-

suddenly a hand covers her mouth

MMMPHHHHHH

struggling

MMMPHHHH!!! MMMMPHHH!!!!!

struggling

she bites her captor's hand

angrily, breathless Any hand gets put over my mouth is fixing to lose fingers. *breathing hard* You have no idea who you are dealing with, Mister. You tell your henchman to let go my arms and get his paws off my bosom and maybe we can talk like civilized folk.

Ah! He's strong! No, don't you approach neither…you…you animal. No.

pronouncing her swords in slow, cold fury Get your hand off my chin … mmmmmphhhhh

she protests angrily into a long forced kiss, his mouth muffling her wrathful words

mmmphhhh mmmphhh!!!

after the kiss, she spits I do NOT like your taste in my mouth, Mister.

SMACK! he slaps her, and she cries out

You! You struck me!

he grabs her, forces another kiss on her

MMMPHH! NNN!! MMMPHH!!!!

she is panting after the kiss

What kind of man has his friend hold a woman while he lays hands on her ... and kisses her?

a scornful laugh A man who's going to be rich? Is that so? You're going to sell me to that mayor? What makes you think you can hold me all the way to Texas? What...what are you doing there? What are you pulling out from under that bed? *grunting as she squirms and struggles* Rope!! I am not some sow you can truss up like a ... wait, get that away from my mouth, you are not gagging me with one of your gloves, you ruffian, I'll speak as I please, you -mmmphh mmmmphhhhh mmmphhhhhh

sounds of her mmmmph'ing, struggling, rustling as she's tied up tightly ...

then her muffled oomph! as they sit her down on the bed

her indignant whimpers for a minute, then the glove is taken from her mouth

she gulps in full breaths, then tries to SCREAM but is interrupted by three sharp slaps across her face: SMACK! SMACK! SMACK!

a tremor in her voice All right. All right, I won't scream. Let's just ... discuss matters calmly now. *quivers* We can discuss this calmly, right?

You've got me tied up, my arms behind my back, my wrists bound in your rope. And you've sat me down on the bed. You've got my face cupped in your hands and your palms are warm against my cheeks. Well I feel all kinds of helpless now, Mister. But it's a right long ride to Houston and you have to sleep sometime, even your henchman does, and I'll wiggle loose and get my Smith and Wesson, and then where will you be? Sharing a flask of whiskey with your Lord and Savior, I imagine.

And anyway, listen. You don't want to sell me down in Houston. That mayor, he's a grouchy old coot. He'll put a noose on my neck, and that'll be the end of me, certain. And you wouldn't want that? A pretty young lady like me, to hang by the neck until dead? Why, so early in life, before I done half the things I mean to? I've never been to California yet. Never robbed a bank. *softly, sweetly, teasingly* Never been touched by a man.

I mean … a vigorous man like you, there must be something you want more than you want eighty dollars. I've seen all night how you look at my bosom. Felt your hands on me, too, when you kissed me at the door. How you gripped me. Your flesh so warm on my naked breasts, under my bodice. My nipples hardened for you, Mister, you must have felt them. What if I let you touch my bosom a while, just warm your hands for a bit. You can kiss me, too. You clearly like kissing me. And this time, I'll kiss you back. I'll moan and whimper into your mouth hotter than any whore in Nevada, and you can just … touch me.

And your henchman there, the way he's staring at me. We could make him watch, you could fondle me and have your man watch your conquest. I hope you're paying him enough. Because when you cup my breasts in your hands, I am going to moan more sweetly than any woman he will ever hear again in his life, you neither. And then once you've enjoyed my body a while, untie me and let me go, and we'll forget we ever met. Except you'll have the memory of my sweet, warm bosom to comfort you on many cold nights.

How about it, Mister?

breathes full and deep

My breasts are heaving for you each time I take a breath, Mister. Do we have a bargain?

I … I'm not sure I rightly understand. Why … why bargain for something you already have? I …

the sound of tearing fabric

a shocked little cry

You've … you've bared me! To my navel. With my breasts bouncing free in the moonlight. Why… Oh! Why you animal, get your meaty paws off me!

panting, gasping, whimpering soft pleas, squirming

No, no. No. Don't squeeze my breasts like that … oh Lord above, your hands are strong. And your man holding me down by my shoulders while I squirm and kick and you have your way with my bosom, that isn't right, that isn't fair, Mister.

breathless I didn't say you could have me yet!

more tearing fabric

Stop stripping me! Oh Lord, you can see my … wait! … you can't mean to … deflower me!

Unhand me!

squirming, more desperate No, no! Your hands caressing my thighs!

panting, desperate Wait, wait, wait! All right, all right, I see you drive a hard bargain, Mister. But if I'm to hang, you don't want me to stand before God in heaven a defiled woman, do you? I have enough in this life to answer for. There's two of you and you've got me tied and you can ravish me, certain. You could shove your glove back in my mouth to keep me quiet while you violate me, and the good folk in the saloon below and in the town outside would be none the wiser, they wouldn't know what you've done to me. You could do that.

But wouldn't you rather have me willing? I could be good for you, I could. I may be virginal and pure as spring water but I'm no fool, I've seen everything in heat from cats to horses to men and I know how the deed is done. I could … I could do that for you, willing and wet as Delilah in the Good Book. Touch you everywhere with my soft hands and my wet little mouth. Welcome you into me. I wouldn't struggle or whimper or nothing, I'd just lift my hips for you and kiss you and make you feel like one of God's own angels. *softly* Could I do that for you, Mister? Give myself to you? Give you my virginity?

Those men I killed. The men I kissed with my Smith and Wesson. You can have what they wanted. What they never got.

You can have me.

And then you'd let me go?

softly Look at my bosom heave for you. Look at my breasts. Look at my soft thighs gleaming with moisture. I have more bounty to give than any mayor in Houston.

breathes May I give you everything, Mister?

Strike a bargain with me. Please, Mister. Anyway I've been a virgin too long. I want this. I want to make this bargain and let you ride me like a stallion rides a filly. All night. I'll be pleasing, I will. Just make this bargain with me, Mister. Please, Mister, please.

Mmmm. Thank you.

You might be no kind of a gentleman, but I knew you were a good businessman.

You won't regret it, Mister.

Would… would you like to kiss me?

a long, deep kiss, with her making sweet little noises into it

softly I won't spit out your taste this time, Mister. You can kiss me as much as you like.

kissing

You have me all night, to have your wicked pleasure in.

After which, you'll let me go in the morning?

Good.

And untie me at sunup and give me my Smith and Wesson back?

You ... you'll bring the gun to me right now? What do you mean, Mister?

a soft little gasp

You're... you're caressing my bosom with the gun. With my own Smith and Wesson.

soft little whimpers

The steel is so cold.

Ahhhh ... when you rub the barrel over my nipples...

moans

What are you doing to my breasts, Mister? *softly* What are you doing to me, Mister bounty hunter?

quivery That gun has taken the lives of seven men and you're ... caressing me with it.

moans My bosom is very sensitive, Mister bounty hunter, and I see you have noticed that and are taking full advantage of it. *gasps!* Kissing my nipple with your warm mouth right after the cold gun has touched my skin. That is not fair, Mister. You are getting me flustered more than any lady should be... *moans*

Ohhh ... Your mouth ...

Why are you lifting my gun to my face... *hushed* ... rubbing my lower lip with the tip of the barrel, cold as an icicle...

frightened Are you fixing to shoot me now, Mister? We made a bargain…

… you … you want me to kiss it?

breathless I … I suppose I could. That gun has traveled far with me, strapped to my hip, and has kept me from being ravished on many an occasion. I suppose I could give her a kiss.

vulnerably You aren't going to shoot me when I do?

quivery All right.

the sound of her kissing the gun sweetly

softly Like that, Mister?

I did not think when I greeted the sun this morning that I would be held down on your bed by your henchman brute who is nearly drooling over me now, with my dress ripped open and my hands tied under me and my breasts bouncing as I breathe and my gun pressed to my mouth for a kiss.

I never thought I'd be captured like this.

we can hear her melting submissively, despite herself Lick it? With my tongue? I…I can do that.

the sound of her licking the gun

My tongue is warm … and wet … and soft. And she is so hard and cold.

licking

her voice stays soft, though just a hint of her sass comes back Is this what you want? Is this exciting you? Licking…and kissing…my gun while you both watch?

kissing it again

a soft sigh Ohh, you're trailing the barrel down over my chin, … along my throat … and it is wet from my mouth. You're making me shiver, Mister.

moans softly Circling it around my nipples like that. My nipples have puckered up, swollen and aching while you tease them.

You ARE a ruffian. A gentleman wouldn't torment a lady so. Wouldn't make her insides clench with heat. Wouldn't make her drip her sweet oils down her thighs. Wouldn't make her fill your room with … with the scent of her arousal.

gasps And the tip of the gun … tracing its way down my belly … *gasps again* … pressing at my navel …

What are you going to do to me, Mister?

quivery, soft whimpers of arousal Ohhh … teasing my inner thighs with it … I know I'm slick with my heat down there, I can feel it.

she cries out as he strokes the gun along her folds

Ohh! I'm so wet there! Don't tease my folds!

Don't…don't shoot me…

whimpers Don't shoot me. This is not how I want to die...

moans Ohhh, you're rubbing me with it THERE. On my soft little button. Oh Lord. Oh Lord. That... that... *moaning*

My thighs are quivering. And my insides are wet heat. What are you doing to me?

Are you enjoying this? Forcing such pleasure on me with my own gun?

whimpers You just keep teasing my little button...

improv her moaning and whimpering as he excites her body

I can't believe this is happening ...

I am a lady. You will not make me surrender. You can have your pleasure in me, but I will not surrender to you in pleasure. That I will NOT do. I will not. You certainly will not make me scream in heat while you tease me with my own Smith and Wesson!

her moans get more desperate

No, no, I don't want to, I don't want to... You can't, you can't make me surrender...

Please, Mister, please...

Stop caressing my button, please, please!

Ah! Your henchman is groping my bosom! Oh God, too many hands on me... Ah! Don't pinch my nipples! No-no! Ahhh, how roughly he squeezes my breasts!

a gasping cry Your mouth on my thighs!

Oh Lord! *she squeals sharply* You bit me! You bit my thigh!

Oh, OH! Your mouth on my ... No, don't lick me, don't kiss me there, AHHHHH!

Your mouth! Your mouth!

he licks and kisses her soft pussy

No-no-no, no-no-no, no, no, NO! Pleeease!

she cums, explosively

panting

softly, spent I surrender.

breathless And you're bending over me…while your henchman fondles me… I have never felt so helpless in a man's grip…

kissing

her moan into the kiss

I…can taste myself on your lips.

kissing

blushing I taste sweet.

whispers Do I taste good to you?

rustling clothes

You're taking off your ... wait, don't I get to rest a moment, Mister? I'm still shaking ... *gasps* ... Oh!

Well, I declare. THAT's what one looks like.

in wonder, her voice quivery Are they all ... big, like that? And thick? Twitching in the night air, like it's just aching to get inside me?

gasps You ... you want to put it WHERE?

In ... in my mouth? While your henchman gropes me, you're going to thrust that into my mouth?

whimpers All of it?

I have seen dogs and horses and dragonflies make love, Mister, but I have never seen one do that. I don't think it is meant to go in my mouth, Mister. And my mouth is MUCH too small for ... Wait, don't grip my hair, what are you doi-mmmphhh mmmphhh MMMMPHH!! MMMPHHH!!!!!

she protests wildly, muffled, around his cock as he fucks her sweet little mouth

the wet sounds of this forceful blowjob

then her gagging

heaving for air I can't breathe! I can't-MMMPHH! MMPHHH!!

more choking and gagging; he is VERY rough with her

heaving for air Are you fixing to choke me? Shooting me would have been kinder, Mister. Please-MMMPHHH MMMPHHH MMMMMPHHHHHHH

more gagging sounds as he takes her throat

muffled protests around his cock

her squeal as he fills her mouth

after a delay, we hear the sound of swallowing, gulps as she resigns herself to swallowing everything he has given her

heaving for air

Heavens! *panting* Heavens!

So much of it.

You tasted like the sea.

You just shoved yourself in my throat and you THROBBED and you poured an ocean into my mouth.

still breathing hard I didn't know you could do that.

slightly defiant, slightly dazed You ruffian. You are NO KIND of gentleman.

SMACK

her shriek

SMACK

Ahhh! Yes, forgive me, I'll treat you with respect, I will. Yes, yes, forgoing eighty dollars is worth a little respect. Yes, Mister. Yes.

What…what do you want to do with me now, Mister…Mister bounty hunter?

gasps Give me to your man, while you recover? What? WHAT?!!

That was NOT part of the bargain!

a cry

Don't you flip me over! No-no-no! I am not to be just HANDED to some hired low-life scoundrel. I promised YOU my virginity, Mister, I … wait, I still get to save my virginity for you tonight? I don't understand. Why … why is your man bunching my torn petticoats up above my waist, then? Why is he gripping and …

SMACK! (the henchman spanks her)

ahhh! … smacking my rear? I don't understand, I …

SMACK!

I am not a wayward child! And I did not agree to be spanked like one! Let me up!

SMACK! SMACK!

Stop! Oh you fiends, what kind of monsters are you, to do this to a lady? Let me go!

SMACK! SMACK!

the henchman starts spanking in her in a rapid, driving rhythm, and for a minute she just whimpers and shrieks at each spank

Mister, Mister! *SMACK!* Please don't let your henchman do this to me! *SMACK! SMACK! SMACK!* Please! Please help me!

improv a hard, long spanking, her pleas and begging protests becoming less and less coherent, until she is just sobbing in little whimpers

he stops, and we hear more clothes rustling

she whimpers You brutes. You brutes.

whimpering Your henchman is climbing on top of me… Is he going to mount me … like a mustang? You promised me, Mister! You promised my virginity was for you, not your hired man! Please! Get him off me! I'm squirming, but he's so damnably big! He's strong!

GASPS!!

Wait! What! What is that? Hard and thick, pressed to my… *a shocked whimper* No, no, not there, not there, that's my ass … not there … not my ass! please … you can't mean for him to take me there!

Please! He can kiss me! He can *whimpers* … spank me more. He can be in my mouth! I'll swallow his seed, too! Please, anything!

He can't take my ass! He can't! Oh LORD he's so big! He's so big, pressing there! Mister, please! It's unnatural! It's

NOT part of the deal! Please, please!!! Don't let him ravage me! Don't let him take my a-

her shocked scream as the henchman penetrates her ass, interrupting her

No!

her shocked cries of protest at each thrust as he takes her

No! No! Don't!

Get out of my ass!

her cries become furious

You animals! How dare you! When I get my guns back I'm going to blow off your brutish cocks! Both of you! How can you let him do this to me! Get him off me!

No, don't you put that glove back in my mouth, you bast- MMMMPHHHHH!!!!

MMMPHHH! MMMPHH! MMMPPHH!!

her desperate cries into the glove-gag at each thrust ... improv a minute of rough, intense assfucking

the glove comes out, and her cries become whimpering moaning half-screams

breathless and defiant Oh, you're hard now, too? You want to ravage me, too!

AH! Lifting me up! I will kick! I'll kick! I'll squirm! I'll struggle!!! Oh no, I'm caught between you, between your hard bodies, so many hands on me, so many hands … on my bosom, on my thighs, a fist in my hair … AH! … If I wasn't tied up! … Unhand me!

No, no, Mister, your cock is at my … no, no, I wanted to give you my virginity sweetly tonight, not like this, not like this, not with two of you in me, please don't…please, you'll hurt me, you'll hurt me, you're so big, he's so big, you're both so damn big, PLEASE-

she screams as the bounty hunter takes her, penetrating her, claiming her virginity

wet sounds

panting Two in me, two in me, two in me…

wild, animal grunts from her as they both fuck her

I'm so full, so full … Oh you animals, let me go! This is NOT what we agreed! Oh, why are you both so BIG! MMMPHHH!

the bounty hunter forces a kiss on her, and she moans and grunts into the kiss

No! No! No! Don't! Ah! Ah! I am so full of your cocks! I am so full of your cocks!!!!!

animal grunts and moans from her … her whimpers of protest, her cries as they both take her … her pleas are mindless with heat and pain and pleasure and with her body's overwhelmed surrender … this is where the voice actress can really sell the idea that she is being completely fucked out of her mind

I can't! I can't! I can't! I can't! I can't!

I feel you th-th-throbbing! Both of you! You're going to … in me! No! NO! Not in me! Not inside me! Not in me! Not inside me! Oh no, no, don't make me shatter too, don't make me squeeze your cock! Don't, don't, NOOOOOO

her anguished cry as they cum in her becomes her own orgasm … and she cums

after, she is just panting and sobbing and quivering, completely undone

gasping for breath

No…don't caress my cheek so gently. Nor my hair. Don't be tender. *a quivering intake of breath* Your henchman is still gripping my bosom, and you're both still IN me. You are not my lovers. You have RUINED me. I want my gun back. I want to be untied. I want your big, meaty cocks out of my soft womanhood … and my ass. I want you to let me go. *sniffle* Please let me go.

What…what do you mean it's not…not dawn yet?

I can't take anymore!

Please! I'm so sore!

You can't do this to me. You are NO KIND of gentlemen! When I get loose, I am going to kill you both like I did the others! I'm going to get my gun back and k-MMMMPHHHHHHHH

Get your filthy palm off my mouth! I'll bite you! I'll-MMMPHHHHHH

MMMMPHHH!!!!

her muffled grunts and wet sounds as they take her again for a minute

she cums again

we hear her whimpered sobs into the handgag after her orgasm as they keep thrusting in her ...

her desperate muffled cry of protest as the thrusts get faster

her smothered wail as the bounty hunter cums in her again

her whimpers afterward

mmmphh mmmphhhh

mmmphhhh-mmmm-mmmm

he lifts his hand from her mouth

tearful, gasping You made me squeal like an animal.

Are...are you ever going to let me go?

You ... you don't even mean to honor the bargain, do you?

You're just going to ravage me every night on the way back to Texas?

quivery Please. I...I'll surrender. Completely. I'll take whatever you give me. Whatever your henchman gives me, too. I'll...I'll squirm and whimper and squeeze you so tightly.

Aren't I tight? And soft?

And wet?

I'll do anything. Just don't … don't take me to Houston.

Please.

I'll… Maybe … maybe I'll give you so much pleasure, night after night after night, that you'll want to keep me instead.

I'll kiss my gun for you. I'll kiss your cock. I'll scream when you both ravage me. Please, Mister. Please. I'll find ways to be worth so much more than those eighty dollars. Let me be your good, wet little whore. *softly* I'll be SUCH a good whore.

kissing, whimpering into the kiss

I'll be your good little whore.

I promise.

the softest whisper, that the listener has to strain to hear Until I can get my Smith and Wesson back and escape.

louder Your … little … whore. Just keep me. Keep me and ravage me.

kissing … her tearful whimper into the kiss

the scene ends

7

Tipsy Elf Maid in a Tavern

TAGS: [F4M] [I Might Be Slightly Tipsy, and a Chaste Elf Maiden, and You Are Clearly a Grunting Primitive Human Beast, BUT You Should Probably Ravage Me] with some [NonCon] [Seduction] [Fsub] [Kisses] [Light Bondage] [Eager] [Wet] [Cunnilingus] [Titjob] [Primal Sex] [Creampie] [Ahegao]

We hear the muted sounds of a tavern and the soft breathing of the elf maiden. She sighs softly, takes a swill of her drink, swallows delicately, then sighs again

What am I doing here? This tavern is teeming with humans, there isn't an elven male in sight, and those candles are smoking something awful. At least the winter ale is good. *takes a little gulp* Mmm, actually really good. Well, that's one thing humans are good for.

sighs This adventure has been a total wash. 100 gold, what kind of quest reward is that? Well, and this little violet I've tucked behind my ear, enchanted so it will never wilt. It's pretty. But the quest reward I WANTED was a kiss. Seriously, is that too much for a chaste but voluptuous elf maiden to ask? I saved that arrogant high elf's life and I SAW how he looked at me, with his eyes like two round moons, and he didn't even KISS me. *mutters* Some gratitude.

takes a swig of her drink, a little more gustily

I'm SURE I'm the best elf archer this side of the crystal forest. And, well, I AM beautiful. And here I am, alone, at a tavern, getting slowly tipsy, surrounded by all these humans drinking and singing and … belching. Oh, what am I doing here? Maybe father was right. I could have stayed home, married some elven merchant with a big purse, and just settled down to give him a baby once a millennium or so. *sighs* He didn't even ask my NAME. He took one look at my forest clothes and the sword scar across my cheek and the dirt smudged on my skin after battle, and he was like, *she imitates his deep voice* 'Well, you aren't QUITE a proper elf maiden, are you?' Yeah, well a proper elf maiden would have just swooned instead of saving your high-caste rump from those marauding trolls, wouldn't she? You could admire your proper elf maiden while they cook you both in a pot. Humph! *imitates his voice again* 'Probably a half-elf.' *mutters* Bet he's half an elf under his belt. *angry little sound*

she takes a drink

sighs He was really pretty, though.

wistful Couldn't he have given me one kiss?

lifts her drink and finds it empty Aaaaand now I'm out of ale. Grrreat. *almost tearful for a moment* It isn't fair! I am NOT tipsy enough yet to deal with the fact that I'll probably still be a chaste virgin when I reach my fourth century.

Am I not pretty enough? My eyes are green as the depths of an enchanted lake, my ears are pointed and so cute, my skin flawless and elven-young, well, except for the scar. My bosom is full and soffft, my hair like silk. I guess my hair WAS disheveled, strands of it stuck to my cheek with sweat, from battle. But ... don't I look ... fetching ... when I'm sweaty? I'm sure I must. 'Half-elf.'

sniffles It's not fair.

the sound of another mug being set down by her

Mmm? What's this? Tavern keeper, I didn't order another drink. I didn't. I spent nearly all my gold at your village merchant, to buy this Breastplate of Superior Agility. Which I THOUGHT was going to be an actual breast PLATE. You know, a metal plate that protects MY breasts. Instead, it's this skimpy little bra of enchanted satin that barely even covers my nipples. Just look. It's such a ... delicate little thing. Little red ribbons and ... *bewildered* ... bows. And just look. You can see the swell of my breasts, their soft cream, moving with each breath I take. And in battle, my lush elven breasts would fall right out of this thing! *she makes a cute, delicate little snort* Some breastplate. *mutters* To say nothing of this Satin Miniskirt of Greater Stealth which barely covers my thighs and isn't even remotely lore-friendly.

Anyway, I clearly can't afford another drink. *sighs* Even if it is foaming so appealingly and ... and it smells like just what I need right now. But I ... I can't. Please, take this drink away and banish it to some dark place where it can't tempt me.

Oh. OH. Are ... are you serious? Someone BOUGHT this drink for me? *a little excited* Oh. Oh wow. Is ... is that like a human thing? A quaint primitive custom of yours? Do humans buy each other drinks?

That man over there? *softly* Oh, he's ... wow, he's ... big. Do ... do humans often get that big? He looks like he could snap Sir You-Must-Be-a-Half-Elf like a dry branch. Those ... mmm, those arms. Wow. *flustered* Whew. It's, it's frightfully warm in this tavern. Don't you have any windows? Oh, he's looking at me. Oh my. I'll just ... uh ... here, hand me that drink.

long, long gulps that go on and on

Whew. Oh, I have ale trickling down my chin, dripping onto my VERY unprotected bosom. Well, that's fetching. Tavern keeper, would you do me a favor and go talk with that masculine behemoth over there, um, and inquire about his name? His parentage? His ... uh ... the nature of his interest in me? Like why has he bought me a drink? And are his muscles naturally all firm and big like that or *blushing* is it some kind of enchantment? Oh wait ... he's *sadly* ... he's not sitting there anymore. Where did he go? Tavern keeper, forgive my incivility but I must leave at once. *clatter* Ohh, I've knocked over the stool. Well! This is not like me at all. I am GRACEFUL! Um, excuse me, I ... I need to go find that ... that male BEAST. And ... oh ... *a tipsy, helpless giggle* ... um, he's ... he's standing right behind me, isn't he?

she turns

Oh, hello, male human person. *blushing* Hi. You … you ARE big. Wow. I … uh … I … I'm Seliana. It's really quite lovely to meet you, and … uh … thank you for that gift of fluids! Um, I mean, not … not fluids, the, uh, drinky thing … that you sent me. Whew, it's really hot in here now. I'm sweaty, aren't I? And my hair's sticking to my face again. Oh, I'm botching this. I'm sorry, I really am very young, barely 350, and … well, I guess you're probably used to the untutored ways of grunting human women, *softly* so anything that comes tumbling from my lips probably sounds like music to you, doesn't it? *low and sultry* In my sensual elven voice?

hopeful And when I … uh … knocked over that stool right in front of you, well, ahem, I'm still probably much more elegant and … refined … and, um, … bosomy … than your shapeless human women, aren't I? *whispers* Get it together, Seliana.

Do … do you have a name?

gasps You've taken my hand? That's … well, that's daring of you, human beast. Ooooooh, and you're kissing my fingers. Wow. Uh. I … uh, I don't know what to think. Um, oh … and my wrist. You have … very soft lips. Very soft. Wow, really soft. Ohhh, how hungrily you kiss me. *whispers* I wonder how those lips would feel on mine.

he kisses her, and she moans sweetly into the kiss

Ohh. You taste like … adventure … and woodsmoke … and MAN. *a soft little sigh* Oh, do that again.

he kisses her and she moans hungrily, muffled by his mouth

in awe Wow. Wow. Your mouth is so wet and so good.

… Are you … are you smelling my hair?

she makes a soft, aroused little sound, and then she takes a little breath

Ohhh, I can smell you too. *she breathes in deeply* Oh wow, your scent. You smell like just what I need right now. Wait, what am I saying? I'm afraid the SIGNIFICANT quantity of your winter ale I've imbibed is … affecting me a little. I … can we sit down? Oh! *her voice goes soft* Oh, you're holding me. Right here, against your unbuttoned shirt and your … very … hirsute … chest. Seriously, is this FUR? What is this? It's like … HAIR! Sprouting from your chest. It's … oohh, it's, uh, really … soffft … *whispers* under my fingers.

Do all humans have chest hair like this? Or were you cursed? *whispers* You aren't a werewolf, are you? That would be AWFUL. Because, you see, I left my bow by the bed upstairs and, well, I have a very sharp knife strapped to my calf, but it isn't silver, and I'm much too tipsy right now, aren't I, and I do NOT want to be torn to pieces tonight, that would be a TERRIBLE ending to an unimpressive day, and, oh, you're not a werewolf, all right, that's good. That's really good. You're … you're holding me very close.

And you have my breasts squished against your chest. *she moans helplessly* And you're kissing my cheek … *gasps* … kissing my scar. You … you really think I'm lovely? *a sweet little feminine sound*

Ohh, yes, your hands are VERY warm on my bosom. And I guess I DO need something holding my breasts to protect them. This Breastplate of Superior Agility certainly isn't doing the job. *moans* Oh, how you DO that. Mmmmm. Sliding your hands under the satin like that, oh, just cupping my breasts. Mmm. Your hands are so warm. Um. Keep … keep doing that. Mortal warrior, you should know, this is a … *moans* … this is a terrible idea. You're a human primitive and … and … and … *mewls* … you have really strong hands!

You, uh, you realize that all your fellow human savages are watching us, don't you? You … you don't care? *moans* Oh, I guess I don't either. By the wells of Evra, your … your mouth on my throat. Oh. Oh wow. I … I can't even breathe. I … I'm only an elf maiden, chaste and pure and delicate, I might swoon!

her garments rustle, and she gasps

Oh! You're carrying me! All right, well, if I swoon, I guess I'm safe.

footsteps

sultry, flushed Where are we going?

the creaking of his feet on the stairs

Upstairs? Where the other feral humans won't see you kiss a girl of the elven race? *softly* Where they won't see you make her quiver? *a short, sweet kiss* Mmm, I really like your kisses. Does it feel good to a human if I kiss YOUR neck?

sweet, gentle little kisses with soft little noises and sighs

I can taste the sweat on your skin. Are you just back from a battle, too?

Giant spiders? Really? You saved a farmer and his family from web-lurkers?

a door creaks open

Mmm. And now you're here, carrying me into my room. Oh! And setting me on a bed. Oh, not my bed. Not my room. This is YOUR bed, isn't it? Why am I in your bed, warrior? Is something going to HAPPEN to me in this bed?

breathless Really? I … I'm YOUR quest reward? *giggling helplessly* You get much better quest rewards than I do.

we hear his belt unbuckle and his garments rustle

Oh! Oh dear GODDESS. Uh … um … that's … that's MY quest reward? I take it back, then. That is a … VERY … big … reward. I really didn't know they came in that size. That is, um, NOT an elven cock, is it? Not elven at all.

rustling

she gasps You're on top of me, you bold beast. *kissing* Mmmph! … I'm very tipsy … and this is happening very fast, and … mmmphh!

he kisses her, and she protests briefly, muffled, into the kiss, and then breathes softly and kisses him back, then moans passionately, muffled

whispers Your kisses intoxicate me more than the winter ale. If you keep doing that, I won't be able to think, or speak, or do anything but whimper. I won't even remember my own name. You've lit flame between my thighs. *an aroused little whimper* How have you done this to me?

he kisses her again, hungrily, and she whimpers in need. We hear rustling clothes

Well, there goes my 'breastplate', you've tossed it on the floor. That's all right. *whispers* It wasn't doing me much good anyway. *moans* Oh yes, cover my breasts with your hands. Oh goddess. *breathing in little gasps and moans of need* Hands of Superior Sexiness. Mmmnn! Yes, warrior, protect my breasts with your hands. Hold them SO firmly. Mmmmn.

Oh wow, I'm wet. I can feel my warm honey trickling down my thighs under my skirt. Oh I am so, so wet. How did you do this to me? You're so … so primitive. So primal … So … ahh! So hungry! Suckling my breast! Oh human! Human! *sweet little gasps of pleasure*

panting Okay, so THAT's what that feels like. Having my breasts suckled by a warm, wet, strong mouth. Mmmn!! And licked! Oh yes! Yes! Lick my nipple. I like it. I really like it. MMMNN!!

the rustling of her skirt

And you're tugging at my skirt. Okay, okay, wow, I … *breathless* … what am I doing? I'm … I'm shimmying out of my skirt, that's what I'm doing. Oh this is really really not a good idea. I'm … *moans* … naked. Except for the … the thingy … *giggling* Whew, too tipsy … um, thingy, the knife strapped to my thigh. *giggly defiance* I still have that!

we hear her knife unbuckled and unstrapped from her thigh and sent clattering across the floor

breathlessly aroused All right, no knife. Defenseless. That's exciting. I'm defenseless and naked in the arms of a ravaging primal BEAST.

You REALIZE you're just a grunting primitive human and you should NOT have your hands on my perfect, elven body? Groping me like this … leaving bruises in the shape of your fingers where you grip me? I am an elf maiden, and you are a feral animal that happens to have the shape of an elf … *quivers* AND really warm hands … *mewls* … and a really, really big cock. *moans* Oh, your kisses on my breasts! Mmmn!

Why… why are you lifting my wrists above my head … crossing them …

we hear the belt buckle

she gasps

whispers tying them in your belt …

You're binding me!

aroused Oh, that belt is tight. *in wonder* I'm tied up. I'm really, REALLY tied up. Mortal warrior, you realize I've slaughtered entire goblin warbands from the treetops, put an arrow through the eye of a dragon in the Hellfrost Mountains, *quivers* and I've never ONCE been tied up.

he kisses her, and she whimpers sweetly into the kiss

subdued, aroused, soft You have me naked on my back, tied up, in your bed. And ... if I wriggle ... *she grunts softly as she struggles* ... oh wow, you really aren't letting me get away at all. I can squirm but ... you're on top of me ... *she gasps and almost squeaks the next words* ... muscling your hips between my soft elven thighs! *moans and squirms*

a tipsy giggle I'm helpless. Captured! *panting in arousal* How did this happen?

teases What are you going to do to me, human warrior?

panting My father DID say I needed to be careful, adventuring in the forest. That trolls would want to eat me, and human savages would want to RAVISH me. That if I wasn't vigilant at all times, some human warrior might CATCH me and tie me up and force himself on me by his campfire in the dark forest night! Is that what you want to do to me, human? Ravish me? Are you going to use me for your pleasure?

Ohhhh your fingers. Right there. *whimpers* On my blossom. Oh, I'm dripping on your fingers. *a soft mewl of need* That stick-in-the-rear high elf was RIGHT. I am not a proper elf maiden.

But ... *kissing* ... mmm, I am ... *kissing* ... chaste. Still chaste. *moaning into another kiss* ... Mmm. Ohhh, you're fondling my thigh. Okay, yes, you can do that, human.

squirming I really CAN'T get my wrists free! *breathing faster* Human, I've ... *kissing* I ... I've never ... *kissing* ... mmm, I mean, I'm a virgin, and ... *kissing* ... 356 years is FAR too long ... *kissing* ... even for an immortal elf woman

... *kissing* ... and, see, my ... my ears are sweetly pointed and my nipples are hard as little berries, and my thighs are warm ... *kissing* ... I KNOW you desire me and ... *kissing* you crave my innocent young flesh ... you want me ... *kissing* ... and I can feel that brutal cock of yours so unforgivably THICK pressed against my hip ... *kissing* ... I am really REALLY tipsy ... *kissing* and helpless *whispers* and DANGEROUSLY wet ... *kissing* oh, do it, do it, you savage, primitive, masculine BEAST ... *kissing* ... take advantage of me ... *kissing* ... take my virginity ... *kissing* ... please ... *kissing* ... please ... mate with me ... *kissing* ... ravage me as you desire ...

panting and moaning and squirming

breathless Come on, do it, warrior. I'm bound and pinned under your hard body! If I scream for help, you can cover my mouth with your hand! Anyway in this tavern, there are only barbarian humans to hear my cries. *a soft little whimper of need* I can't stop you from plucking my innocent elven flower! Take me as roughly as you take your uncultured human women! Rut in me!

breathless Use me!

panting, slightly frustrated No, really, ravage me. It's taking an awfully long time for you to rape me, human male. And it is UNSEEMLY to make an elf maiden of the eternal forest beg for her deflowering! Especially at the rough hands of a rutting animal. Why are you kissing your way down my belly like that? Aren't you supposed to thrust your cock in me? You're ... you're just breathing in my scent, between my thighs! That is REALLY embarrassing, human beast.

Having you just SMELL me like that, where my petals are naked and spread open by your fingers, *whimpers* and barely hidden at all under the soft, silky hair between my legs. What are you ... *a scream of shock and pleasure* ... you BIT me! You ... you animal!

panting And your lips ... you're kissing my ... *gasps!!!!* ... my mound! My soft mound! And my ... my ... my ... oh GODDESS! *squeals* You're LICKING me THERE! Wait! Wait wait wait!

moaning and squirming

desperate My elven pussy is FAR too sensitive for your warm ... wet ... BRUTISH ... human tongue! I am not one of your coarse human females, you brute! My petals are so soft! I can't possibly bear this ... this ... this sweet torture! You have to stop! *squeals* Oh dear goddess! I can't ... I can't ... So hot ... So hot!!

moaning Oh, your mouth is magic! Better than any enchantment in the elf-woods! I've found another thing besides ale you humans are good at! I'm tied, I can't stop you! Lick me! Lick me as MUCH AS YOU LIKE, MORTAL!

improv her breathless arousal, cunnilingus, her sweet little cries

wild with her approaching orgasm I ... I ... I'm going to surrender! You have me tied up and you're LICKING me and I'm going to surrender, I can't believe this, I can't believe it, I ... I ... I surrender! I surrender! I surrender!

cries of orgasm

her voice soft and amazed afterward Oh my goddess. OH my goddess. 356 years was ... MUCH too long to go without that.

whispers What you DID to me.

You're climbing on top of me ... straddling my chest. Oh, that cock is BIG. Oooh, yes, take my breasts, mmm, squeeze them together. OH by the seven moons. You're sliding that hard, hot cock between my breasts.

whispers Oh wow.

Does that feel good? My full breasts, their soft, soft caress along every inch of your cock?

she starts to grunt very faintly as he thrusts

amazed and aroused and amused all at once You are RUTTING between my breasts. Mmm! You ARE an animal, just like father said. Mmm! Mmm! You're so rough! Just rolling those hips and rutting on me! Oh that cock is so hard between my breasts. You're making the bed creak!

Does this feel good? Does this feel good? Using my breasts?

You ... you want ... what? You want me to spit on your cock? Get your cock ... wet and sloppy? Is ... is that what human women do?

softly I'm your tied elven captive. I'm not in any position to refuse. *sultry* No matter how you choose to degrade and defile my virginal elven body.

Yes, lift your cock toward my face. *gasps* You smacked my mouth with it! You brute! *gasps as he does it again*

she spits loudly

Again?

All right.

she spits a few times

Wow, your cock just … THROBS as you stroke it, rubbing my spit up and down your shaft. Oh yes, slide it between my breasts again. Mmm, that feels so strange. Your cock wet and hard and brutal between my breasts.

You're … going to cover my mouth and 'fuck my tits'?

Ah! Ah! Mmmphhhh!

she grunts, muffled, into his hand, as he fucks her breasts hard and fast … her soft little grunts get faster

he stops after a little while and lifts his hand from her lips

she takes in a gulping breath of air

You've made a sweaty mess of me, warrior.

Yes, I'll … I'll kiss it.

kissing warmly, wetly

I'll kiss your cock.

another wet kiss

then, rustling, and she cries out Ah! Flipping me onto my belly? Why … why? *whimpers* You're on top of me, so fucking big. Oh my GODDESS, I can't move at all. Ah! You're pulling my hair! And your cock is RIGHT THERE! At my flower! No-no-no! NO! You can't mean to rut in me from behind! YOU may be a primal savage, but I am an elf maiden! I am not an animal! You can't DO this! Let me up! You - MMMMPHHH!!!!

he covers her mouth and she protests haughtily, muffled under his palm

she squeals into his hand as he enters her

wet sounds

we hear her muffled moans and grunts as he fucks her hard on the bed, on top of her, his hips pounding her … she squeals and moans and cries out into his hand as he gives her thrust after thrust after thrust!

he takes his hand from her mouth

a wild, passionate, desperate moaning cry, explosive from her lips once his hand is removed

I can hardly breathe! *panting* You are so BIG in me! So big! Human! Human!

grunting wildly as he takes her

You animal! Just taking what you want from me! Just taking what you want! *she cries out* Your fist in my hair! Ah! What are you - MMMPHHH! *he kisses her savagely, and she moans helplessly into his kiss panting* You brute! You brute! I'm so wet! I'm clenched around you so tight! Tied up and raped by a human ANIMAL!! Do it to me! Do it to me! *she squeals* You're SO DEEP! How can that cock be so BIG in me!

improv her moans and squeals, rough primal sex

Yes! Yes! YES! Show me what a human male can do to me! Break me, human! Break me! Fuck your tipsy little elf girl! MMMPHHH!

he covers her mouth again and takes her wildly

he lifts his hand

barely able to speak, for pleasure You ... you know my elven father ... he would ... he would kill you for doing this to me ... you know that, right? *squeals* Yes, grip my breasts! Squeeze my breasts! Bruise me, warrior! Claim me! I NEEDED this, and I never knew!!! I .. I ... I wanted a kiss ... and I'm being TAKEN by a hard, human ape!

Rape me! Rape me, human! Oh goddess oh GODDESS oh GODDESS! *squeals* Yes, twist my nipples! *screams!* Pound me! DESTROY me!

I'm going to surrender again, I'm going to flood your cock! I'm going to drench your cock! You're, you're ... what, what, what? No, no! Not inside me! Not inside me! Wait-wait-wait-WAIT! Cum on my breasts! Cum on my breasts! You will NOT spawn in me, you beast! I am an elven woman, you do NOT get to breed me! You do NOT get to pump me full of your seed! Get off me, get off me, get OFF m-MMMPHHHHH!!!

she squeals a wild protest into his hand, then screams into his hand as she cums, as she feels him cumming inside her

afterward, we hear her soft little whimpers muffled under his hand

then her soft breathing

at last he lifts his hand

just above a whisper You filled me.

trembling Don't you know how fertile elf women are? *trembles* You've filled me with a child, human warrior. I … I wanted a kiss … and you filled my womb.

she moans Oh, you're pulling out of me. *whimpers*

she pants softly for a moment or two

softly I feel your hot, sticky seed leaking out of me.

whispers Oh my goddess.

My thighs are still shaking … from that orgasm.

What … what is happening to me?

he kisses her, and she whimpers sweetly into his mouth

softly I was a virgin, and you took me. Not as an elf lord would, with song and reverence, but like a brute in the forest. *whispers* And I'm still so wet. What you made me FEEL, warrior.

a nervous giggle What are you doing with my Breastplate of Superior Agility? *gasps* Tying my bound wrists to the bed!

What ... what ... wait ... *a soft little moan* Mmmmm, when you grab my breast like that ... mmmm ...

Okay, now your sweet elf-captive is tied TO the bed. Oh, you've stood up and you are just ... LOOKING at me. Oh your eyes are hot. Here, I'll roll onto my back so you can see me better.

squirming sweetly See me wriggle for you. Here I am. Your Seliana. Your tied, well-fucked little elfgirl, my wrists above my head, my legs open wide. I imagine my soft elven pussy is swollen and red from how roughly you took me. My breasts bounce as I squirm. *squirming*

Wait, ... where are you going?

Downstairs to get more ale for us? You can't LEAVE me like this! What if someone else comes in?! What if the tavern keeper comes?!

No, don't take my Satin Miniskirt of Greater Stealth with you! Don't! I know it barely covers anything, but I need it! You can't sell it for ale! I won't have ANYthing to wear! You animal! *panting*

...You're going to bring the ale up and then rut in me again. Is that so? *squirming* Well, maybe I won't let you. I AM an adventurer. A trollslayer! A hunter of the woods! Maybe I'll get to my knife. Maybe I'll get free! MMMPHHH!!!!

he kisses her, and she squeals into the kiss, then surrenders, moaning passionately into his mouth. It is a long, hot kiss.

breathless and submissive All right. Kiss me like that, and you can do anything to me tonight.

another passionate kiss

Mmmm. I'm still going to squirm loose, though. *squirming and whimpering sweetly on the bed*

footsteps, and the creaking of a door opening

passionately Don't be long! I'm bound to your bed and so WET! Don't be long! Please! Please!

the door shuts

we hear her soft breathing

I've been ravished. I've really, really been ravished.

By a human male.

squirming And I'm tied … so tightly … to his bed.

whimpers And I can feel his cum trickling out of me.

so softly What's going to happen to me?

squirming

Wow, he tied me well.

breathing a little faster And he is so … so vigorous. …

You animal. You just mounted me and TOOK me.

softly Come back, human. Come back. My thighs are soaked.

I'm really NOT a 'proper elf maiden.' *whispers* I feel like such a wet little animal. My clit is aching for your touch. And the whole room SMELLS like me. Like you MATING me.

tipsy giggle Oh, hurry back.

Take me, human. Ravish me. *whispers* Fuck me all night.

we hear her squirming sweetly against her bonds

the scene ends

8

This Wounded Elf Priestess Needs You to Heal Her With Your Cock

TAGS: [F4M] [Wounded Elfgirl] [Friends to Lovers] gentle [Fdom] [Devotion] [Cunnilingus] [Blowjob] [Tenderness] [Size Difference] [Hot Sacred Elf Sex] [I Need Your Sexual Healing] [Passion] [Creampie] [L-Bombs] [Love Bites]

sounds of fire crackling in the distance. The ragged breathing of the wounded elfgirl.

a gasp of fright

then a sigh of relief Oh, it's you. My bodyguard, my protector. In the starlight, I thought you might be one of the slavers. But it's you. Climbing the broken steps of my temple, to kneel by me, where I lie crumpled on the stair. Oh, my faithful warrior. Beautiful human. All my spells are used up, all my life is spent. The slavers are slain, the city deserted. We are the last. *a ragged breath* The children of Asha, you got them away safe? You got them out of the city?

Oh, you have done so well. *an exhausted attempt at laughter* My sister elves told me I was a fool to hire a human for my bodyguard. A grunting savage, they said. He'll paw you in your sleep. He'll piss like a dog on the temple floor, or sleep at his post. They're beasts, animals, those sweating humans. That's what my sisters said.

Oh, they were so wrong. Our young novices, all those sweet girls, would be dead tonight or sold into slavery if it weren't for you. *trembly* You have done so well, human male. I did NOT make a mistake when I hired you.

The enemy thought I'd hidden the elf-children here in Asha's temple. And I stood at the door, letting no one through. They threw soldiers at me thick as arrows, while the city burned around us. But it didn't matter how many attacked. I am the high cleric of Asha, and my spellcraft is strong. I tore up buildings and crushed the slavers, I summoned wind, I called fire, I lit flames in their loins until they fucked each other and rolled about rutting on the ground. Any who set foot on the temple stair, I destroyed.

trying to breathe normally, clearly in pain Oh, but it cost me so much.

How you look at me. My pointed ears, my eyes tearful from pain, reflecting the starlight. My hair sweaty across my face, my gown half torn from me and bloodied, my breasts quivering as I fight for my last breath. I am a mess, mortal. And these wounds, where my wild magic has torn open my own body.

she cries out in sudden pain Oh, you're lifting me. *wincing* Be careful, my warrior. I am weak now.

tearful My body is dying. I gave everything I had. *fiercely* No. You do not get to regret. Don't. You came back to me as soon as you could. My wounds are not your fault! I gave you the order to leave me. To get the children away. Oh, tell me the children are safe. Tell me I did MY job well. Please. Before I die, tell me …

listens

whispers Thank you. … the children … they're in the forest now, hidden in the tree boughs, but you could hear them singing in praise as you ran back to the city? You … *sobs* … you heard them singing my … my name?

softly They should sing YOUR name, my warrior. You got them away. I was the distraction. Tearing up the streets with my magic.

crying softly with pain and exhaustion and relief

You're carrying me into the empty temple? Oh, good. Yes. I'll rest my cheek on your shoulder. *a soft, feminine sound* This feels good. Mmm.

the sounds of flame fade. We hear water trickling as they enter the temple.

It's quiet in here, and lovely. These marble columns carved like slender aspen trees, the fountains of clear water, the tall goddess beneath a ceiling open to the stars, bare-breasted, palms open in welcome. Carry me to her, my warrior. Lay me at her feet. Please. This is where I should die.

her whimpers of pain as he sets her down

Gentle, gentle. Oh, my body. *tearful* My beautiful body. 920 years I have lived, an elf woman, in service to my goddess, and my body remains elven-young and lovely in the starlight. But it is time for me to leave it now. *sniffles* I didn't even get to see my first millennium. But I do not regret. We … kept the temple children safe. We did that, together. You and I, my loyal, beautiful man.

You're … are those tears in your eyes? *gently* Do not grieve for me. You're human. I … I danced in this temple as a laughing girl, I knelt and gazed up into Asha's marble face and begged to be a cleric, centuries before your family tree began. As much of it as you can recall. Human, I have lived a good life. Full of … love and passion … and my goddess has been so kind to me. *whispers* I do not regret.

her ragged breathing for a moment

the rattle of armor cast aside

the tearing of cloth

softly What are you doing, warrior? Throwing your armor to the floor, ripping your tunic and undergarments into strips. You're trying to bind my wounds. Oh, lovely human. It is useless. You have protected me all your adult life. From werewolves in the dark, from vampire assassins, from goblin raids. There's nothing more you can do to protect me now.

Unless.

whispers No. No, it's unthinkable.

It is my time. *whispers again* I do not regret.

No, do not ask me. I am delirious with pain or I wouldn't have said … wouldn't have hinted. I … I can't. Elf clerics don't … do that … with humans. Not usually.

No, you're right, nothing about tonight is usual.

she hesitates Asha forgive me if I wrong you in telling you this. You have seen me heal wounded elves, the elegant males of my race? My goddess is kind, and by her gift, I can steal an elflord from the edge of the grave, mend a mortal injury. I clasp him in my arms and welcome him into my body. I sing Asha's prayer, and in our cries together, his hurts are healed. He has new life, new fire blazing in his blood. I give him that.

You have seen me, and my sister clerics, do this?

There is another mystery of Asha, one you have not seen. If … if one of her own clerics is wounded … which does not happen often, because we are not warriors … but, if it does … then a virile elf-warrior, unwounded and vigorous and strong, can mate with her, spill a gift of hot, gushing life into her body, giving her strength for one last healing spell, that she may use on herself. It is a great honor to save an elf-cleric from death. To be inside her, clasped tightly within her, moving in her like a god, restoring her.

But this is a thing that elves do.

I could not … I must not … ask a human male. To give that to me. To caress my body from the inside and heal me. I could not ask it.

My fingers touch your cheek. Beautiful male, you are mortal.

I don't even know what it would do to you.

softly Have you ever been inside an elfgirl? We are tight, and our cunts burn hot as the fire inside the Earth. What if you gave me too much? What if I drained some of YOUR life? You have so little, I couldn't bear it.

Oh, you weep for me.

Don't ... don't do that.

Bring your face down here. Come here. I command it, human. Let me kiss the tears from your cheeks.

she covers his face in soft, sweet tears, quivering with passion and tenderness

Besides. I might break at a touch.

a pained but happy laugh Willow woman, you call me? I bend like a willow but do not break? *sighs* I might tonight.

Yes, human, I know you are naked. I am not unaware. You've torn off all your clothes, to tend to me. And you look ... good, naked. *aroused* That mortal cock is ... brutally thick. And ... so beautiful. You don't ... you don't mind me looking? It's hard not to look.

I have seen you naked before, you know. Mmm-hmm. When you bathed in the sacred pool behind the temple.

amused How you gasp! You thought no one was watching. This is the temple of Asha, silly man. Some sweet elfgirl is always watching. And YOU were using OUR holy pool. *giggles* A grunting human savage in Asha's waters. You're lucky it was me who saw you.

I stood on my balcony listening to the stars and breathing in the night air. I heard a splash. I looked down. There you were! Your muscles rippling like a god's as you cut through the water. I couldn't even breathe, watching you. I pressed my thighs together, but my warm honey still trickled down my legs. Oh, what you did to me that night, and you didn't even know it. I tossed in my bed until dawn, biting my own hand to keep from crying out, fires of Asha burning in my cunt, and my soft little fingers labored to put out the fire inside me. But no touch of my hand could ever be enough to quench what you lit in me.

My sister clerics are right. I am a fool. I did dream of … finding some excuse to ride into the forest with you at my side. Of finding some quiet glade. Of letting this gown that is now torn and bloody slip from my shoulders, from my breasts, over my hips, down my smooth legs to pool at my feet. Of dancing naked for you. Of lighting fire beween YOUR thighs. I did dream of that. Of having that effect on such a primal, masculine, human beast as I saw swimming in that pool by starlight.

What? *startled* You saw ME bathe? When? How?

In my bedchamber? You heard a woman's cry from the bottom of the stair, and ran up, stealthy and silent, sword in hand, to protect me? But when you came in and tiptoed across my outer room, there were no signs of struggle, no drops of blood on the floor. But while you stood listening, I cried out again, your name on my lips. So you eased open the door to my bedchamber, gazed in at me in my private bath, my back to you, one slender hand on my breast, the other between my soft, soft thighs.

I am … blushing. You saw me touching my soft petals. You heard me cry out your name.

whispers Why didn't you come to me then?

Were you afraid, because I am the high cleric, and I do not rut with human animals? *softly* Did I sound reluctant to … rut … with a human warrior, when I squirmed and moaned in my bath? Did I sound like I would reject you, like I would banish you from my side, if you stole into my bath and kissed me?

softly I am not the only one who has been a fool.

hardly daring to breathe Kiss me, human warrior. My time is short. Send me to my goddess with the taste of your mouth on mine. I will moan your name, warrior, the way I did as I bathed. I'll moan your name into your mouth as you kiss me.

Mmm. Kiss me.

he kisses her

she moans sweetly, helplessly, into his mouth

the kiss is long, and she makes small, aroused noises as they kiss

breathless You do not taste like a wounded elflord. You taste … mmmmmmm *she kisses him again a sweet, sensual kiss*

panting softly I like how you taste.

trembles Your mouth on my neck. Kissing the line of my jaw. My throat. Do you feel my pulse beneath your lips? *a shuddering, passionate breath* What are you doing, warrior?

rustling garments

How ... how gentle your hands are, peeling my torn gown away from my breasts. Did you get to see these, while I bathed? You said I had my back to you. Look at them now. My breasts are soft in the starlight. They are full ... and lush ... and my nipples are swelling, aching in the cool night air. *gasps* Oh, your breath on my nipple is warm. Oh, you warm me. This ... this is unwise. My beautiful human, this is ... not a good idea. *she moans passionately* Your mouth on my nipple is so wet, so warm, so good.

moaning

yearning I hurt with every breath, but I don't want you to stop. Kiss my breasts, warrior. Suckle my nipples. I am weak, but I can get my fingers in your hair, pull your head close. Ohhhhh, suckle me! Oh, I am a fool! How I need you, mortal!

gaspy little breaths as he touches her

Open ... open my legs? Are ... are you sure? Are you SURE? I do not want to coerce you. It is NOT part of your duty as my bodyguard to pleasure me, or to give me life, only to protect what life I have. And there's so little of it left. Just say the word, and I will release you of your duty, send you on your way. *moans* You don't have to do this for me, mortal.

quivers What are you saying? *emotional* There's nowhere in the world you desire to be but at my side? When you say things like that ... *quivers* ... my hot elven cunt clenches. Everything in me is tight and hot. Oh human, I have craved your touch. I have lusted for your mouth on me, night after night, and I didn't dare speak. I will speak now. A woman dying may say anything she pleases. I want you. I crave you. I NEED you. I want you in me like I want air to breathe, water to drink.

Your touch, the smoldering fire in your gaze, it gives me strength. I will work one ... last ... magic. With you. Will you mate with me, human? Here, at the feet of my goddess, in the most sacred temple of the elves, will you slide your cock into me and make me scream your name?

moans I want to scream for you.

I am opening my legs.

a moan of pain

Oh, oh, my body is so ... so sore. Such violent spells tore through me today. Mortal, help me. Help me open my legs for you. Please.

Yes, yes, like that. *wincing, then a soft sigh of need* There, lift my tattered gown above my hips. Yes. Oh, my thighs are parted. *breathless* You can see ... all of me. Does my soft elven flower glisten in the starlight? Do you see how wet I am?

Do you smell my heat? I am flooded at the thought of your cock.

Please. Please, human. Maybe you are not even here, maybe I am dreaming. *moans* Touch me as you have touched me a thousand times in my dreams.

moaning

Your fingertips are so … gentle.

Yes, yes. *whispers* Yes.

panting I am the high cleric of Asha. I have never lain on my back for a man's touch. If I were well and whole, I would pin you under ME and ride you like a stallion in the desert. I would ride you until you scream to your barbaric human gods! *panting* Oh my barbarian, touch me. Heal me.

humming softly, a sweet melody

It is the love-prayer to Asha. I will be soaked for my goddess one last time. And for you. Do you feel me? *moans* So wet, so wet. Slide your finger inside me.

a squeal of pleasure

hardly able to speak Oh, that … that … yes, like that. *moaning*

she tries to sing again, quivering and moaning as he fingers her

Get me wet. Get me wet for your cock. Get me so ready for you, human.

singing between gasps and moans and quick breaths

a shuddering cry Your mouth! Your lips, your tongue! You're tasting me! Tasting me, tasting me! Do I taste sweet? Do I taste sweet? *she sounds like she is about to come apart* Does my elven honey taste sweet and good in your mouth? Human! Human! What you're doing to me, what you're doing to me, what you're DOING to me ... I ache, my whole body aches, but don't you dare stop, don't you DARE. Lick me, lick me, lick me ...

she tries to sing again, breathless, but her song lapses in a cry of pleasure

she cums

afterward, she is panting softly

whispers Oh, human.

breathing in gasps

quivering Bring me that cock.

Here, to my lips.

Yes, now. I command it. I am wounded; I can't get to it myself. Bring it to me. Bring that hard, masculine cock to my mouth. Please. I want to taste that hard cock you're going to put in me. Give me that cock.

Oh yes.

licking

Does my tongue feel good, curling under your shaft? This is a ... human ... cock. Much larger than I'm prepared for.

sultry Will it grow larger yet? If I lick ... ? *licking*

If I kiss? *kissing his cock*

If I ... suck ...

improv a gentle, sensual blowjob, little whimpers around his cock, whimpers from her body's pain and her body's pleasure.

My mouth is soft and sweet. Enjoy my mouth, you passionate human beast.

sucking

passionate Oh, the scent of you. That primal male musk. If I die tonight, I will die smelling your hot, thick cock.

sucking

And tasting you. *breathes the words lovingly* My warrior.

sucking

whispers If I die tonight, let it be with your cock in my mouth.

a long, intensely sensual blowjob

Mmm mmm. Yes, touch me. Touch me while I enjoy this cock. *whispers* Touch my breasts. Oh, put your barbaric human hands back on my breasts. *moans* Squeeze my breasts.

moaning around his cock

her blowjob gets hungrier

finally, after a while, she pulls her mouth free

Your balls are tightening. We have to stop.

licking his cock

Though I don't want to stop.

I don't ever want to take my mouth off this cock.

sucking for a moment, then a soft hungry little sound as she lets his cock fall from her lips

For the wild enchantment to work, for me to heal, you must be inside me when you cum.

soft and low Put it in me, warrior. I am ready.

My nipples are swollen from your mouth. My thighs are open, and trembling with need. Here … I'll reach down and … ahhhh … open my flower, spreading my petals with my fingers. Look, human. Look. I am so wet and so small. See this soft, tight opening for your cock? I will milk your cock. Oh, warrior.

It will hurt if you lie on top of me. My body's wounds. But, you can hold your weight up on those powerful, muscled arms and thrust in me gently and kiss me. Feel my fingers trace their way down your chest … to your thighs … ohhh, to the soft, soft hair between your thighs, oh warrior, you feel so wonderful. This cock is so beautiful. So warm as I curl my fingers around your shaft. I'll guide you inside me. Like I'm guiding your cock where it belongs. Like I'm welcoming you home. My warrior. Yes, right here. *soft, so soft* Right here. This … this is my soft elven pussy. *quivers* Push it inside me. Thrust your cock in me. Only, be gentle with me – ohhh!

she cries out as he slides inside her

a few wild little gasps

when she is able to speak: I ... I didn't know ... it would be so ... *gasps* ... so big. So big in me. This hard, human cock. *quivering* No wonder my elven sisters tried to warn me. *moans* Oh my goddess. *moans* Slow, slow. Please, please, for the love of the goddess, go slow. *moaning*

Oh. Oh, wow. Let me ... let me get used to you. *a helpless, breathless giggle* My body hurts too much to shift my hips. Will you ... will you shift yours, beautiful man? A little higher? Ah-ahhhh! Yes, oh Asha, yes, yes, YES. You ... you may thrust now. I command it. Thrust in me! Help work this magic in me!

moaning

Human, human!

I can't even ... I can't even think ... I ... I ...

moaning, overwhelmed

Oh, you are so good. So warm in me. So warm. So THICK. *squeals* Oh, my goddess!

Kiss me, mortal.

lovingly Kiss me, my warrior.

a passionate kiss while he rides her in gentle, deep thrusts. We hear her cries smothered by his mouth.

trembling, almost tearful with joy My goddess is kind. I shattered the invaders with my spells, I saved her children, the novices, and now ... now she rewards me. She is giving me you. And YOU are kind. Oh human, so kind. And so strong. Moving in me so gentle ... *moans* ... and deep!

Oh human, human. I don't have words for how your cock feels in me. I don't have words. How you fill me. So gentle, so hot ... don't ever stop moving in me like this. Oh human! My nails dig into your back.

moaning

Forget what I said, cover me with your body, crush me with your love. I can bear it. I can bear anything for you. Already I feel the goddess surging in my blood. Oh, oh. All of me is hot and so full of life. I'm so full, so full.

a wild, gasping cry You're so heavy on me! So big! It doesn't matter, I can take it, pound me. Pound me. Pound that cock in me! Feel my heels grip your legs and pound me, pound me, pound me! *screams*

I will NOT die tonight. *panting* Not with your cock in me! I will fuck, and I will FUCK, and I will live!

squeals Fuck me, warrior. Fuck me!

her moans get wild and hot

What you DO to me! Come here, you beast!

kissing him ravenously. The rustle as she rolls him under her.

You're underneath ME, now. Feel my nails dig into your arms. You beast. I will ride you! Here on the temple floor, by starlight! Oh goddess, yes! Goddess, give me the strength to RIDE this man, to TAKE his seed! Feel my hips roll! And swivel! And fuck! Kiss me!

she growls into the kiss, in her need, and she bites him

Yes, I bit you. Beautiful man. I have to taste you. There is nothing in the world as hungry as an elf woman in love. Ohh, that human cock of yours … how it stretches me. Oh my goddess.

Improv hot, passionate sex

Feel my body grip you. I told you I was tight! I told you I was tight!

grunting each word as she slams herself down on his cock Oh fuck, fuck, fuck, fuck, fuck, FUCK!!

panting Human! I'm going to … I'm going to … fuck! H-hold me close, hold me close, yes, yes YES, bite my breasts! Bite me! Ah! Ah! Human, human, finish the spell, please! Save me! Heal me! Spurt all that hot semen in me! Cum in me, human, and the goddess will seal my wounds, and I will lie in your arms hot with life and hot with love all night! *moaning* Every night! My bodyguard! My protector! Oh I can't hold … any … longer! Cum in me! Cum in me! I command it! I'm squeezing your cock! Cum inside me NOW!

screaming in orgasm

afterward, almost sobbing from the intensity of it

Oh, oh.

Kiss me.

kissing, long and sweet, her soft aftershock-moans muffled by his warm mouth

quivers And … you're all right? The magic we made together didn't hurt you? Your hair isn't any grayer. You don't look MORE mortal. *trembles* I'm glad. I'm so glad.

kissing

so softly Oh, human.

I'm shaking. That … that was … I don't have words for what that was. I've never been so wet! And how you came in me. Such … magic. How you fucked me. Here, in the most sacred temple of my people.

kissing

whispers Your cock is wonderful in me.

Mmmm, I'm going to keep your cock snug and warm in my soft elven cunt. I don't want to let your cock go just yet. Mmm, human beast.

MY beast.

whispers I love you.

You know that, right?

softly I've been in love with you since I saw you in that pool. *amused* Which blasphemy, by the way, you more than made up for tonight by saving the life of Asha's priestess. I think the goddess has forgiven you, human male.

Look. I'm healed. There are just scars where the wounds were, delicate lines on my belly, on my side, on my hip. My elven skin is no longer as smooth and perfect as it has been for nine hundred years.

Oh? You ... think I am beautiful with my scars?

Well, ... *tenderly* ... you're loyal.

Mmm. I think they're lovely too. These scars are my reminder of the day we saved the elfgirls together. And the night you gave me your cock and your heat and shared your passion with me.

You are so sweaty. *giggling* Just like the other clerics said. A sweaty, human beast. Mmm.

whispers I suppose all that sweat is my fault, though. I rode my protector hard tonight.

kissing him lovingly

No, I don't care what the others say. I am the high cleric of Asha. You came back for me. While my city burned, while my blood stained the temple steps. I thought I was going to die alone. You carried me in here, gave me back to my goddess, and she gave me you.

in wonder and gratitude She gave me you.

My gentle barbarian.

In nine hundred years, a woman finds a lot to regret, but I will never regret this.

a sweet sigh You saved me.

Mmm, now lie still, my warrior. I command it. No, don't try to get up. You will do as your elf priestess says. You have fought all your battles tonight. I am going to kiss you … and kiss you … and then, I am going to kiss your cock.

whispers I'm going to kiss your cock for a long, long time.

Feel my soft hands cupping your face. Oh, my warrior. I feel as vigorous as a human tonight. And so hungry. My love. Taste my mouth.

kissing him

I love you.

kissing him

I love you.

kissing, long and sweet, then she hums a little of her love song again, her holy spell

I love you.

kissing

The scene ends

9

Queen of the Red Seas

TAGS: [F4M] [Pirate Queen] [Barbarian Warrior] [Seduction] [Erotic Dance] [Sultry]

inspired by the pulp fantasy of the 1930s

as the scene opens, we hear sounds of battle, blades clashing; the creak of timbers, the splash of waves against the sides of the ship

Take him! He's only one man. He's the only one left of their fat, low-in-the-water barge! Cut him apart, and every man in this crew gets a share of the treasure. Come on! Take him down, as you love your queen! You, you, and you, rush him!

more ringing of steel

a soft catch in her breath Ishtar and all the gods, my deck is strewn with bodies. Stop!

the ringing of blades ceases

I said STOP! Put up your blades. NOW. No one is to touch this warrior! I will speak with him.

her footsteps across the wooden deck as she approaches the warrior breathless By Ishtar, I have never seen your like, though I have ranged the sea from the coasts of Zingara to the fires at the bottom of the world. Where do you come from?

pause I don't believe THAT. You are no soft Hyborian. You are fierce and hard as a gray wolf. Those eyes were never dimmed by city lights; those muscled arms were never softened by life amid marble walls. Who ARE you, warrior? I have never seen one like you. I have never seen a man fight like you. Where are you from? What country makes men like you?

Ahhhh. Now that's better. I like your name.

I am queen. Look at me, warrior! I am queen of the red seas. My fathers were kings. My mothers were warrior-goddesses. I have plundered the seas. I have burned villages and cities and left fleets flaming like dying torches on the water. I was born in the desert and I have walked veiled in cities older than your kind and have walked naked on the waves of seas on the other side of the world. And never have I seen a man who can fight as you do. You have left me with fewer crew, warrior. Look at you. You magnificent beast. You wolf from the high snows, you tiger of the North.

Here, let me touch your arm with my fingers. Do not my fingers burn your skin? It is the desert heat you feel and the fire in my heart. Let me press your arm down. Lower your blade. You could drench my deck in blood, but to what purpose? The ship you protected - everyone is dead.

breathlessly Everyone but you.

And I do not want to destroy you. You are so beautiful. Do you not find me beautiful also? To the men of this crew, I am a goddess. Here. Let me press nearer … nearer.

gasp Ah.

whispering, for his ears alone

I feel your blade brush against my hip. I do not fear it. I do not even fear your other blade, though I see it … thick … beneath your garments.

You will need to wear less on my ship, under the fire of the sun where we will sail. See? This veil about my hips is all the clothing I wear. Mmm, feel my breasts press up against your chest … ah, the way my nipples brush across your skin. They are hardened. Do you feel the beat of my heart? Do my breasts drive a beat of fierce passion through you? Do I make your pulse beat like a drum in the forests? Do you feel my rich black hair where it has fallen across your arm?

Look at me, warrior.

I am untamed as the desert wind.

I am supple … and dangerous. As a sea panther.

There are parts of the world where just my name makes men throw down their swords and cities surrender their walls.

But … mmmm, here … ahh … I feel your sword rising. You haven't thrown that sword down at all.

whispers Am I doing that, warrior? My breath warm … and soft … on your throat? My breasts pressed to your body? My fingers … touching … cupping … gripping …

Mmmm. You may keep THIS blade, warrior. You may even unsheathe it later. But throw down the other.

a ringing of metal falling

Oh, my good warrior. *panting softly in arousal* Take me and crush me with your fierce love! Go with me to the ends of the earth and the ends of the sea! I am a queen by fire and steel and slaughter – be my king!

whispers Say yes. Say yes.

a little cry of joy Ah! Sail with me! We will love, laugh, wander, and pillage! N'Yaga, tend to the warrior's wounds! The rest of you, bring the plunder aboard and sink that sea-heavy ship! And you, my warrior, my northern tiger, my beautiful wolf, gaze on me.

Watch me.

I will dance for you. I, daughter of kings. My wolf of the blue sea, see my mating-dance.

See my eyes burn like a she-panther's as I toss away my sandals. One, then the other.

And this veil about my waist … we will not need it.

I let it slip away to the deck.

And these jewels at my ears and my throat and my belly, gold plundered from islands I left burning like the stars, I do not need them this hour. I toss them clattering to the deck. To my deck.

I will dance naked for you, warrior.

I will dance naked and you will watch.

See the queen you have chosen.

See the goddess of the blue seas and the red.

See the woman you will hold in your arms tonight.

Yes, that's it. Throw your armor to the deck. Stand before me. Let me see your muscled thighs. Let me see that magnificent, hard cock. Let my crew see what a warrior their queen has found! Let them see how well you will please me!

Mmmm. Watch me dance. Like the spin of a desert whirlwind, like the leaping of a quenchless flame, like the urge of creation and the urge of death. Warrior, oh my warrior! Watch my breasts bounce and leap for you! Watch the flash of my warm, wet cunt! My feet spurn this blood-stained deck and every man on this ship has forgotten death and bloodshed as they gaze on me. Have you? Does your sword thicken and rise for me, warrior? Do you yearn to crush me in your arms? My wolf? My tiger? My king?

watch in your imagination, see her dancing, her teasing

her wild cry of heat and need

Oh! With a cry I throw myself at your feet.

panting

Take me, my king. Worship your queen.

she cries out

Yes! Ah! Take me in your arms! Let my crew see their queen accept her lover! Press me beneath you, naked and hot and yours, while the sun sets and the white stars come out above your head. You are bloodied and sweaty from battle, and you smell so like a man … ah, Ishtar yes, yes, spread my thighs … ohh, your hips are so muscled … and your blade, your cock …

goddess, so hard against my folds. So hard.

panting

Do you feel how wet I am?

I will give you the ocean, my warrior. I will give you the sea and all its plunder. I will flood you with its pleasures.

Do you feel me rocking my hips for you? I want you in me, warrior. I want you so deep in me. I want you to take all of me. All of me. Make me your queen.

crying out as he penetrates her

Yes!

Yes!

You are so big. So big inside me. Oh my wolf, yes, ride me. Ride me.

moaning passionately as he takes her

kissing, biting, fucking

I'll bite your shoulder, your chest, I'll scratch my nails across your ass, I'll lift my body and my breasts and my thighs into your thrusts. Oh goddess. My warrior, my warrior, my bloody king. Take me. Take me. TAKE ME.

hot, hot sex; her moan as she rolls him onto his back on the wooden deck

Now that I've rolled you under me, I will ride YOU, my warrior. You are a wolf, but I am a panther of the seas. Oh goddess yes. Feel how tightly I grip you. Mmm. Feel my cunt ripple as I squeeze you. I know how to ride a man. I have made kings captive before and I have made them beg. Will you beg for me, warrior? Will you beg for your release? Will you beg to fill me with your seed? Ahhh. Yes, I am lifting your hands to my breasts. Squeeze me. FEEL me. I want you to devour me, and I want to devour you. I will ride you until the stars are faint again and the sun is rising and I will NOT let your blade slip from its wet, warm sheath until I am satisfied. You serve the Queen of the Red Seas, now.

she rides him, moaning

Oh my goddess. Oh Ishtar. Oh, so big. So big. Do I feel good to you, too, warrior? I can hear your growls, your groans, I can feel you throb inside me. Ohhh. Beg me. Beg me to let you fill me. Beg m-mmmmmphhhhh

he is kissing her hard, ravenously, and she moans hotly into his mouth.

a rustle as he rolls her beneath him

Oh!!! You aren't going to beg, then. *her voice breathless and sultry and near cumming* You're going to capture me beneath YOUR body. Is that how it is going to be, my king? Are you going to ravish me? Are you going to tame me? Are you going to fill me with your hot, thick … seed?

her desperately aroused cries

Mmmm. Yes, that is a sweet, sweet groan you make. You feel my fingers stroking you just behind your balls, teasing the little rosebud of your ass… I wonder what would happen, my warrior, if I pressed my fingertip inside there, inside the warm, soft tightness of your ass. Yes, moan for me. Moan for me. What would happen if I sunk all my finger into you, just as you are sunk into me?

Yes, moan for me. Cum for me, because *I* decide it. Release your seed in me, warrior. Fill me. Fill my cunt. I am a queen by fire and steel and slaughter, and I submit to NO ONE. Give it to me, NOW.

their orgasms rush upon them

panting afterward

Mmmmm. … You are so, so sexy when you cum, my warrior. That groan of yours… ahhh. Ohhhhhh, I want to hear it again.

And again. And again.

Oh, look at your shoulder. My lovely, beautiful warrior. All those scratches, and the blood where I have bitten you.

You are my wolf, and I am your young tiger-cat.

kissing

Mmmmmm *moaning softly into the kiss*

My warrior.

We will make the seas red. We will fill this ship with plunder, and you will slay my enemies and bring me pendants of gold and diamonds for my fingers and ruby teardrops for my ears. And you will heat my bed and you will have a goddess in your arms every night. And warning drums will beat in the forests when they see the dark outline of my ship. They will hear that the she-devil of the sea has found a mate, an iron man whose wrath is like a wounded lion's. And survivors of butchered ships will name me with curses, telling tales of the dark queen and her warrior with the fierce blue eyes; and the cities on the shore will remember us long and long, and our memory will be a bitter tree bearing fruit through all the years. They will never forget us, my warrior.

Mmm. I smell the burning wood of that old barge you were protecting.

breathless And I smell you.

Mmmmmmmmm, I love how you smell.

Do you hear the waves? The creaking of my ship? Do you hear the aroused sighs of my crew, watching us? Do you feel how wet my soft, tight cunt is still, wrapped tight around your cock, mmm, a hot wet sheath for your blade? Oh, my king.

It is deep night, my warrior. I will ride you again now, or you may capture my wrists and ride ME for a little while, until I squirm free and roll you on your back again. You are strong, my tiger, but I am quick and lithe … and wet. So, so wet. Kiss me again. Kiss me while my crew watches my new lover please their queen and their goddess. Kiss me and fill me again, while we rock on these waves and the stars dance above us, hot and naked as I. Mmmmmm.

kissing

I am queen of the dark coast. You are so deep inside me. And I am yours, and not even the gods will separate us.

Take me and please me again, my warrior. *whispering* Take me.

Take me.

Take me.

Lust After Battle: Soldier Girls and Swordmaidens

10

Elf Girls

TAGS: [FFFFFF4M] [Rescued by Hot Elf Women] [Hot Sweaty Elf Sex] some [Gentle FDom] [Good Boy] [Teasing] [Paladin, Ranger, Rogue, Druid, Sorceress, and Cleric] [Blowjob] [Throatfuck] [Titfuck] [Light Bondage] [Outercourse] [Mindfuck] brief [Breathplay] [Night of Relentless Pleasure] [Creampie]

After so much time among sultry elf women, maybe you might like six sultry elfgirls all taking care of you at once, beautiful human.

It is time to form a raiding party of elfgirl warriors. On this raid, meet:

VANNA, *a brave, voluptuous, golden-haired paladin*

ELENA, *a sneaky, sexy, slender raven-haired rogue*

SASHA, *a fiesty, fiery, redheaded sorceress*

ALTARA, *a confident, hungry, silver-haired ranger*

KAI, *a wild, primal, dominant, green-haired forest druid*

CELDEA, *and a graceful, teasing, elegant brunette cleric*

As the scene opens, we hear the sounds of battle, the twang of bowstrings, the clash of blades, women's battle-cries, running feet

VANNA THE PALADIN. Let none escape!

ALTARA THE RANGER. I've put arrows in half of them already! My bow has taken down dragons; these goblins don't stand a chance!

ELENA THE ROGUE. I've got one in a trap-net! Squirmy little beast!

KAI THE DRUID. *she lets out a triumphant war whoop* They're fleeing! Cowardly goblins!

CELDEA THE CLERIC. If I saw your druid vines coming after me, Kai, I'd run too.

KAI. *wicked laughter* Since they like tying up captive elfgirls so much, I give them a taste of their own medicine. And my vines NEVER release their captives.

SASHA THE SORCERESS. They do run fast. I'll put up a wall of flame in their path.

flames

SASHA. Gotcha.

bowstrings

ALTARA. There. That's the last of them. They'll never attack an innocent village again.

VANNA. Well done, girls. Do we have any wounded?

CELDEA. You don't have wounded. You have a healer.

VANNA. Don't get cocky, Celdea.

CELDEA. Goblins are cocky, I'm competent.

ELENA. *gasps* Over there! Look! There's a human!

SASHA. We have to save him!

VANNA. He's chained to a tree. The goblins must have held him captive. Elena, get those cuffs off him.

ELENA. I'm on it!

rattling of a pick in the cuffs' lock

ELENA. *softly, in the listener's ear:* Don't be afraid. I'll get you out of these, lovely human boy. There isn't a lock on this continent that Elena the elf rogue can't pick.

CELDEA. Is he hurt?

ELENA. I think so. He's trembling.

the cuffs open

ELENA. *softly* You're free, human boy. Oh!

VANNA. Is he … ?

ALTARA. He's blacking out.

KAI. What did those goblins do to him?

VANNA. Celdea.

CELDEA. I've got him …

their voices fade to murmurs, then silence

after a brief pause, we hear Celdea the Cleric singing softly, maybe humming without words, a song of comfort and healing. We hear the sounds of a gentle forest pool, ambient forest night sounds, gentle splashing. The elfgirls are in the water with the listener. Celdea and Vanna are holding him.

their voices are all slightly aroused

KAI THE DRUID. The area's clear.

VANNA THE PALADIN. Well done, sister.

ELENA THE ROGUE. *quivery* Good. I'm not up for another fight! Celdea's pleasure-spell is still having … quite an effect … on me.

ALTARA THE RANGER. *moans softly* On all of us.

SASHA THE SORCERESS. And this human male is so cute.

ELENA. How old do you think he is? 300? 400?

VANNA. He's human. Just a few decades, I imagine.

ALTARA. *gasps* Oh, he's just a baby!

ELENA. The sweet boy!

KAI. *amused* 'Baby.' *sultry, hungry* He looks like a grown male to me.

CELDEA THE CLERIC. *stops singing* He's coming around.

ELENA. Poor human.

ALTARA. They must have been so cruel to him.

SASHA. Filthy goblins!

CELDEA. He's safe now.

VANNA. Safe with us.

KAI. *smirking* We're not 'safe.' *her tone goes low and sultry* We are wild. And dangerous.

CELDEA. Kai! Don't scare him with your feral druid ways.

ELENA. He's been through a lot.

SASHA. He's endured so much.

CELDEA. We have to help him. He's a civilian. … Human, are you awake? Open your eyes, mortal boy. It's all right. Don't be scared. Goblins captured you, but we saved you! Open your eyes. That's a boy.

ELENA. Ohhh. He has beautiful eyes!

KAI. Those ARE lovely eyes. You have fire in your eyes, mortal.

CELDEA. Yes, it's night. The stars are out. YOU were out for a while.

ALTARA. You're naked in the water with us.

VANNA. We had to strip away your tunic to bathe you ...

ELENA. ... and touch you ...

CELDEA. ... and tend your wounds.

KAI. *teasing* We're naked too, mortal. Our armor's on the bank.

ELENA. *softly* We're so ... so ... naked ...

SASHA. ... naked ...

ALTARA. ... naked ...

CELDEA. ... we're naked ...

VANNA. Our full elven tits glisten in the starlight.

KAI. Our nipples are swollen and aching.

SASHA. Our smooth legs ...

ALTARA. ... our sleek thighs ...

CELDEA. ... our silky hair, soft to the touch ...

ELENA. ... barely concealing our slick elven pussies ...

KAI. Our HOT elven pussies.

ALTARA. We have to be naked …

ELENA. … and wet …

VANNA. … for Celdea's healing magic to work.

CELDEA. Here, I'll lift this cup to your lips, mortal. Drink it. It's elf honey. Warm and soothing.

VANNA. Drink it all, darling.

SASHA. It will renew your strength, mortal.

KAI. You should feel honored. Few humans ever get to taste an elf woman's warm honey.

CELDEA. It's my honey, human boy, trickled into this cup from between my thighs.

ELENA. And mine.

ALTARA. And mine.

VANNA. We all trickled our honey into the cup.

KAI. We teased our wetness into the cup with our fingertips … *moans*

CELDEA. *whispers* … so wet …

SASHA. Or licked each other until we flooded …

VANNA. For you.

ELENA. For you, beautiful boy.

CELDEA. Our nectar will heal you.

ALTARA. Make you hot and hungry with life.

SASHA. Please drink our nectar.

ELENA. Please.

VANNA. Taste us.

SASHA. Taste us.

ALTARA. Drink our warm … elven … honey …

CELDEA. Our honey has been blessed by the goddess. *whispers* Drink. … There you go.

SASHA. That's it.

KAI. You sweet boy.

CELDEA. Let our honey excite you. Let the healing waters of this pool caress your legs, your body, your balls.

SASHA. … while my hands caress your chest. I'm no cleric like my sister Celdea here, but I have magic of my own.

VANNA. Press close, girls. Touch him. Celdea's already sung the spell. His wounds will close if we smooth them with our fingers.

ELENA. *softly* I don't mind having my hands on him.

ALTARA. Mmm, I don't either.

soft little moans and caresses

KAI. What about my mouth? Can I heal this cut on his shoulder with my mouth? *licking and kissing*

ALTARA. He's quivering. Is he scared?

CELDEA. I think he's aroused.

SASHA. I know he is.

ELENA. *gasps* Something touched my thigh, under the water!

VANNA. That's his cock.

ELENA. It can't be! It's … *flustered* … so big!

CELDEA. Human cocks are like that. Almost … uncomfortable … for an elfgirl. I, uh, had to heal a human ambassador once. I remember.

ALTARA. Celdea, are you … blushing?

KAI. Never thought I'd see that.

CELDEA. It was a very memorable cock.

ELENA. *breathless* So is this one.

VANNA. Human, you are truly blessed.

CELDEA. Here, just relax in the water with us.

SASHA. *sultry* Just feel our soft hands ...

KAI. *moans* Our mouths ...

ALTARA. *moans* Our full breasts ...

ELENA. *moans* Our bodies ...

SASHA. Lush ...

CELDEA. Naked ...

KAI. *whispers* ... and wet.

VANNA. You've been through so much, human boy. We're going to take care of you now.

ALTARA. We'll take such good care of you.

ELENA. We promise.

CELDEA. Just relax.

SASHA. Breathe.

ELENA. Oh breathe, beautiful boy.

VANNA. We're going to make everything better.

KAI. *primal* You're going to remember this night in the forest pool with six naked elf women for the rest of your life, tasty mortal. Let me just rake my nails down your chest...

SASHA. Oh, how he moaned!

ELENA. *quivers* I love the way he moans!

ALTARA. Me too!

CELDEA. Tell him who we are, sisters. Tell him who's rescued him.

ELENA. Human, I'm Elena the rogue, slender and stealthy and soft in the alley shadows. I freed you. I am a sensual thief, stealing kisses in the dark, stealing pleasures too sweet for the daylight. I am a sexy assassin, slaying virgins with the tight grip of my pussy. My hair is raven dark and my lips are full ... *whispers* ... and open. For your mouth. For your cock. My breasts are small and sweet, not voluptuous like Vanna's. Just ... a handful. *whispers* Put your hands on my tits. *moans* Oh, mortal. Yes, hold my soft tits. Mmm. Feel my mouth at your neck. *kissing* My pointed ears quiver with need.

SASHA. With passion. I am Sasha the sorceress, from the summer plains, where the elven tribes ride to war on the backs of lions. I wield battle magic, windstorm and wildfire. I work with heat and flame. I have traveled so far. I joined my sisters here to scorch goblins out of the world. There is fire in my hair and fire between my thighs ... *whispers* ... and I burn for you tonight. My tight elven cunt burns for you.

VANNA. I am Vanna the paladin. From the elven cities, from the gleaming towers of the dawn. My hair is gold, my breasts full and perfect. I cup them in my hands for you. I lift my tits to you. Do I excite you? I am brave in battle and in bed. In combat, my blade catches the sun. In love, I ride my companion until he gives more seed than he ever knew he could. I am a paladin and pure, and you may not breed me. But I will wear your semen on my tits like a badge of honor. I will stride into battle with your cum drying on my body under my armor. What greater reward could I seek than to know I rescued and protected and helped heal a wounded man, freeing him from captivity and seeing his body awake and hot with life? It is why I fight. I will never let you be captured again. Kiss me, mortal.

a sensual kiss, and the others moan softly

ELENA. Oh, his skin is so soft. How can a mortal's skin be so ... soft?

KAI. Ohh, and yet ... his cock is so hard, throbbing in my hand. Do you like my fingers, mortal? My fingers small and soft ... *whispers* ... and insistent, stroking your cock? My eyes are green and hot? See the green of my hair? My body is wild with all the heat and need and lush vitality of our green world. I am Kai the druid, of the deep, deep forest. I am the summoner of wolves and hawks, the screamer in the oak. When you taste my mouth, you will taste the OLD forest. I bind enemies in my vines and bind lovers in my bed. *whispers* Do you want to be bound?

ALTARA. Don't scare him, Kai.

ELENA. *surprised* No, he ... he does want it. Look at his eyes.

KAI. I felt your cock throb for me, mortal, when I mentioned bonds. *whispers* Put your hands behind your back. Good boy. My good boy.

sound of water splashing, then weeds binding him

KAI. There is green life even under the water. These weeds winding about your wrists will hold you tight for me. You're tied up. Helpless. Ours.

VANNA. His cock! He's growing as you touch him, Kai.

KAI. *purrs* I know he is.

ALTARA. Oh, look at it!

VANNA. Erect as my battle-blade.

SASHA. Oh, my thighs quiver.

ELENA. May I … may I touch him too?

KAI. You may, Elena. I'll share.

ELENA. *softly* Your cock is so warm. Mortal, sweet mortal boy. I'm so glad I freed you. I had no idea how handsome you'd be.

ALTARA. My arrows slew most of your captors, from my bow strung with the hair of a virgin goddess. I am Altara the ranger, my hair elven-silver, the irises of my eyes white like snow on the Hellfrost mountains. My bow curves like the winter moon and my arrows are sharp. I have hunted werewolves and ghasts and dragonkind with their wings that eat the stars at night. And I have hunted men. *softly* But I do not hunt them with arrows. Look, mortal boy. I'm parting my thighs. Look at my pussy glisten. I am so wet for you.

CELDEA. We all are, each of us naked in the water. I am Celdea, cleric and healer, from the temple of holy Asha. Vanna is voluptuous, and Altara is sharp like an avenging hawk, and Sasha has round hips and eyes that burn, and Elena is slender and small and feisty, and Kai …

KAI. Kai is wild.

CELDEA. *giggles* Yes, Kai is wild. I … I am gentle. And graceful. My hair soft and brown as a gazelle's. My legs long. My lips sweet. My tits high and pert. I am a dancer. I have danced the love prayer many times. I danced it on the edge of this pool when Kai and Vanna carried you down to the water. And at my prayer, the goddess has lit desire inside each of us, and we drip with need. Tonight, I have made us all sister healers for a brief time, we six immortal elves, to bring you back from whatever torments the goblins did to you. Oh, mortal. We blaze so hot with lust and life that our very touch can heal. By reminding your cute mortal body to throb with life. Elven healing is very … intimate. You don't mind, do you, human? My fingers trace this scar on your chest. Do you feel the warmth of my touch? What if I … press … my cunt to your thigh? *whispers* Do you feel my warmth? Do you want to … fuck … an elfgirl, a cleric of the holy goddess?

ALTARA. Let me kiss your neck, mortal. *kissing*

VANNA. Your shoulder. *kissing*

ELENA. I will kneel in the starlit water and lick your thighs. Here, where the water laps against your legs. *kissing and moaning*

CELDEA. I will lick your ear. *licking*

SASHA. Your neck. *licking*

KAI. And I … will weave my fingers into your hair, turn your head, and take your mouth. *a feral, ravenous kiss* That is how an elf druid kisses her mate in the wild forest. Do you want more, mortal?

kissing

Mmm, I'll untie your wrists. Just for a little while.

we hear the bonds coming loose

You'll want to touch us. *whispers* You'll really want to touch us. *teases* I'll tie you up again later.

wet kisses and sweet wet sounds from all of their mouths

CELDEA. Feel our fingers … our hands …

ALTARA. Our warm little tongues …

VANNA. Oh, mortal. Your body is so …

KAI. … male.

ELENA. *breathless* I want to kiss his cock.

they all moan

ELENA. I'm on my knees, the water licking at my tits. Gazing up at you like I'm in heat. I'm a thief, I'm good at finding places to hide things. *giggles* Hide your cock in my mouth.

Mmm-hmm. That's right. This tight elven assassin with the raven hair is going to lick ... *licking* ... and kiss ... *kissing* ... and moan around your cock. *soft blowjob sounds, and her muffled moan, so sweet and needy*

Is my mouth good?

sucking

And wet?

sucking

Do you like being in my mouth?

sucking

Do you like having a sexy little elf rogue suck your cock?

sucking

Mmmph. Mmmphh. *teasing* Maybe I'll get you off. Maybe I'll make you cum in my mouth.

sucking

Would you like that?

sucking

Would you like to fill my mouth with your hot, sticky cum?

sucking

Is that what you want, human?

sucking

You want to cum in my mouth?

sucking

Mmmm, wow, I could suck this cock for hours. It's heavy and warm on my tongue. Oh, this cock is so perfect for my small elven mouth.

sucking

whispers Here, hide your cock deeper in my wet little mouth!

sucking

suddenly, a squeal of surprise

Oh! You've … you've grabbed my ears! My pointed elven ears! ah! ah! ah! Mmmphhh mmmphhh

intense blowjob sounds

gasping for breath I think you're getting your strength back, mortal! Mmphh! Mmmphh!

blowjob sounds

panting Yes, you can fuck my mouth, you can fuck my – mmmphhh mmmphhhh

intense blowjob

SASHA. Here, sister. You've had enough. We must all take part in healing him.

ELENA. *a moan of protest around his cock ... then breathing hard* But ... but ...

SASHA. Come on.

ELENA. *a groan of protest* Hmmph. Human, I ... will steal you later. *she kisses him, then whispers:* I really like how you taste.

SASHA. Elena is a sweet, tiny thing who will wriggle like a cat in heat if you fuck her. She'll scratch and bite like a cat, too. But. I ... *whispers* am fire.

She can't take you as deep or hot as I can. I will SWALLOW your cock, squeeze it with the muscles of my throat until your body remembers EXACTLY why it's good to be alive. You won't need to hold MY pointed ears, mortal. With this hot redheaded sorceress sucking your cock, you won't even remember what your hands are for. All you'll be able to do is move those hips like a good boy and MOAN.

Now, let the healing start. Kiss me. I want you to kiss this mouth that's going to fuck your cock.

the kiss is fiery and passionate and she moans into his mouth like she is going to devour him

breathless Good boy. Now ... *sultry* ... let's make some MAGIC!

I'll kiss my way down your chest ... mmm

kissing

… your belly …

kissing

… your groin …

kissing

Oh, how you smell. Oh, that masculine human musk. So overpowering. Whew!

giggles Now GIVE me that cock.

sudden intense, deep blowjob sounds

she sucks and sucks, vigorous and urgent

choking sounds

panting I … I … I might have miscalculated.

ELENA. It's NOT an elven cock, sister. He's human. And big.

SASHA. *breathing hard* FUCK. … Human, I don't care. I can do this. I am so wet. When your cock hits the back of my throat, my elven pussy just clenches. I'll go down on this cock until my nose is pressed to your groin, your balls soft against my chin. And then I'm going to stay down like that and gaze up at you with my wild elven eyes hot as fire, and I am going to just swallow. My throat will convulse around your cock. I am going to milk your cock. Watch me!

several moments of throatfucking sounds

then sounds of her swallowing loudly, just forcing her throat to convulse around his cock

VANNA. *awed* Wow.

CELDEA. *awed* Sister.

ELENA. *defiant* I ... I am going to learn to do that.

SASHA. *heaving for air* Your cock! Your cock!

she goes down again, all the way, and makes those delicious sounds with her throat

then she comes up, panting

ALTARA. Oh, he's enjoying you.

KAI. *amused* He really is.

VANNA. *amused* Sasha. Didn't you say we have to share him?

SASHA. Oh, all right, Vanna. *panting* You have a really good cock, human.

VANNA. My turn. I'll kneel in the water, too. Full-bodied and womanly. I am a paladin, and I am here to serve. Let me just ... tease your cock with my fingertips. So gently. I need to keep this throbbing cock ... warm. And protected. *laughing with soft delight* I have an important question for you, human boy. Have you ever wanted to titfuck a paladin? Mmm. Now's your chance. Put your cock between my tits, human. These full tits will envelop your cock. You are going to fuck a voluptuous elfgirl's tits. Mmm, that's it. Feel how soft, how SOFT, my breasts are. I'm holding your cock so warm and safe between my tits. I'll press them together and bounce a little. Oh, oh. There we go. Yes, mortal, thrust your hips. Fuck my tits. Fuck this paladin's noble, sexy, creamy tits!

for a few moments, her aroused little noises

Here, let me get my tits wet.

we hear her working saliva in her mouth

she spits

There. Saliva dripping down between my tits.

CELDEA. Give him more of it. Elf saliva has curative properties for mortals.

VANNA. *laughs* EVERY part of my body has 'curative properties.' I am lush, mortal. *sultry* And yours.

more spit

There. That should make it slick and wet between my tits.

Go ahead, sweet human. Put your cock between my tits again.

moans

Oh yes. Oh-oh-oh. Oh, that cock. Oh, that big warm cock. My tits are bouncing for you. Fuck my tits.

Oh, look, mortal, look. My golden hair falls loose about my breasts. Brushing teasingly over your groin. Oh, mortal, fuck my tits. Fuck my tits.

moaning softly

You are so hot, so hot!

Do my tits feel good? Do my soft elven tits feel GOOD around your cock?

Oh yes, yes, yes. Thrust your hips! Yes! I'll lick the tip of your cock. I'll lick! Mmm! Mmm! *licking* My wet little tongue! Mmm! Mmm!

improv her soft moans and gasps and licks as she gives him such a sexy titfuck

I am an elfgirl of the cities of the dawn! Golden-haired and good and giving. Let my breasts give you such pleasure!

grunting softly, sweetly as he thrusts

ALTARA. My turn, dear sister.

VANNA. Ohhhh. *reluctantly* All right, Altara, all right. I would have let him cover my tits with his seed. My neck. My face.

ALTARA. Soon. Here, mortal. I am going to put my arms around your neck. My lips so, so close to your mouth. *kissing him* Mmm. Beautiful mortal. *kissing* Gaze into my mountain-elf eyes, the color of snow. Human. I'll press every inch of my warm body to yours. Do you like my tits too? I know you must. Your cock throbs against the inside of my thigh.

Here, I'll reach down … Feel my fingers curl around your cock, strong and sure. I am a ranger, skilled at woodcraft. And sexcraft. I once tracked four elf-warriors home through the hills to their bedchamber of ivory and silk … *whispers* … and fucked them all that night.

I always know what I'm hunting. I always know what I want.

I want your cock.

whispers I need it.

Here. Right … here.

whispers This is my pussy.

This is my tight … wet … elven pussy.

Nuh-uh. You're not going to thrust it into me. Not yet. I'm just going to slide … ohhhhh … my soaked pussy back … unnnh … and forth … along your cock.

whispers I'm just going to get your cock wet.

moans You feel so hard, so warm and so good. Oh, so good, so good, so good. *moaning* Sliding along my wet petals. Oh, oh. I'm dripping my honey down your cock. Do all mortals feel this good? Oh, you beautiful human. Human! Human!

KAI. *amused* Careful. You might CUM on his cock.

ALTARA. *moans* Ohhhh, I wouldn't mind! He can have as MUCH of my warm honey as he wants! *her voice goes hot and intense* Human, grab my hips. *moans* Oh, I like your hands! Just grip me and FUCK the outside of my pussy. *moaning*

That's it! Slide that cock along my slit. Yes, yes, yes! Oh you good boy. Oh you good boy. Oh YES!

her moans continue through the lines that follow

KAI. Well, it's my turn, but ... I'm not going to stop her. Here's what I'M going to do, lovely human. I'm going to take your hands ... no, you don't have to hold her hips. Altara is perfectly capable of fucking herself silly rubbing against your cock without your help.

ALTARA. Oh, I am! I am! So capable! *moans*

KAI. *amused* Yes, human, cross your wrists at the small of your back, just like that. *giggles* Good boy.

the sound of the weeds binding him

whispers Tying you up again ... just like I promised.

Mmm. When I tell you something's going to happen to you ... *whispers* I make very sure it does. A druid of the wild wood keeps her word.

Now, I'm going to press my body to you from behind, green and hot, while my sister presses her tits to your chest and her pussy to your cock, so I can tease ... *gasps* ah, you're going to tease MY thighs with your fingers? My tied-up little boy? *moans* Oh, SMART boy. You keep doing that. *moans* Feel how wet I am.

exhales Feel my breath warm on your neck. *exhales*

I'll reach between your magnificent thighs ... take your balls in my fingers. Mmmmm, there we go. I'm just going to caress … and massage … and SQUEEZE …

ALTARA. *moans*

KAI. *giggles* Oh, how you throb! My sister liked that reaction. Mmm. So did I.

Altara's moans continue softly as Kai speaks in the human's ear, moaning softly herself

KAI. SUCH nice balls. … Now while she teases your cock like she wants to make you spurt your sticky hot semen all OVER her naked thighs, I am going to caress your balls … *whispers* … and mindfuck you. I'm going to lick your ear … *licking* … and whisper. I'll tell you what's going to happen to you once my sisters have healed you and enjoyed you. Mmm-hmmm. You get that cock all hard and hot and ready to burst, rubbing it on my sister's soaked cunt, and you … listen. You … just … listen … like a good boy. Because after you cum for my sisters, I'm going to take you away with me. Mmm, that's right. Deep into the dark forest. Elena, that little cock-thief, wants to think she's freed you, with her lockpicking skills, but. *whispers* She's just stolen you away from the goblins for MY pleasure.

I'm going to take you to my cave beneath the willow tree, tie you tightly in unbreakable roots, and I'm going to use you, night after night after NIGHT. *whispers* My … toy.

Uh-uh. Hush now. I'll cover your sexy mouth with my hand. You get to speak when I tell you to speak. Mm-hmm. That's a good boy. Just whimper into my fingers. GOOD boy.

whispers I like how you whimper.

You're going to whimper a LOT for me. I might use you as furniture. As a FOOTstool. Or I might leave you bound for a WEEK and just use your hot little mouth between my thighs whenever I itch to be fucked. You won't get your cock in me. Just … your … tongue.

whispers Did you like drinking our nectar? I will GUSH my dark nectar into your mouth, human male.

And if I DO let your cock inside me, you might not survive it. *softly, intensely* It will be like being fucked by the forest. Wild. Passionate. Destructive. THAT's what kind of elf woman I am, beautiful boy. My cunt will destroy you, I will leave you wrung dry and sobbing with pleasure. Feel my pussy wet against your fingers? My sister's, wet against your cock? How you groan! Feeling alive and ALL better, are we? Poor hungry mortal boy.

Shhh. I said hush, human.

whispers Don't cum.

Don't … cum.

Here, feel me pinch your nose shut with my thumb. I'll take your air, your breath. Mmm. Good boy. That's it. Just squirm. Feel my fingers teeeeease your balls. Good boy.

You get to breathe when I SAY you get to breathe.

Mmm-hmmm. You just fuck the outside of Altara's sweet ranger-elf pussy and you squirm for me. Squirm, human boy! The elfgirls have caught you! I KNOW you want to breathe. I know you FEEL the burn of it.

But not ... yet.

Let that cock THROB. That's a boy. Oh, your balls are so tight! Do not cum. Do NOT disappoint me, mortal.

Good boy, good boy. Mmm, there. I'll let up. Take a breath. Mmm-hmmm. And another. Good boys get to breathe.

whispers Bad boys get whipped by a green elfwitch and fucked until they scream.

Are you a good boy or a bad boy?

giggles I'm going to find out.

whispers Once my sisters are finished, you're ... all ... mine.

You think about THAT while they ride your cock, hot little human boy.

I'll let go of your balls now. Remember ... don't ... cum. *whispers* I'll tell you when you get to cum.

ALTARA. Unnh! Unnh! Unnh! Oh, human, human, I'm going to ... I'm going to ... I'm going to cum on your cock! I'm going to cum on your cock! I'm going to cum on your cock! *screams* Beautiful human boy!!

she screams in orgasm

KAI. *laughter*

ALTARA. *panting* Oh, wow. I've ... I've soaked your cock. I came SO hard.

KAI. Mmm. You're really flushed, sister.

ALTARA. *panting* I'm never going to track four elf-warriors through the hills again. *hot with afterglow* Fuckkk! I'm going to find four thick-cocked human warriors!

KAI. *amused* Aw, your nails scratched up his shoulders when you came. You're supposed to be mending him, not scratching him, sister.

ALTARA. I couldn't help it! Oh, you've made me a wet little animal, human male!

CELDEA. *gently* Girls, it's time. Time to finish the magic, the healing rite. All of you, slip your delicate, soft fingers between your thighs. Touch your heat. Ignite the fire.

they all moan softly

ALTARA. Oh, we are already really fucking ignited.

CELDEA. *laughing* Elfgirls, burn even hotter!

ELENA. *whimpers* Gladly!

KAI. Mmm, I like this idea.

SASHA. Oh yes!

ALTARA. Oh goddess!!!!

VANNA. Oh, I ... I ... I REALLY like my fingers.

CELDEA. Sweet tied-up human boy, I'll take your arm. You're safe. I am a cleric of the goddess of love and healing. Come with me to the edge of the pool, while my sisters writhe and moan in the water.

we hear splashing sounds as he goes with her, and soft moans from the other girls, luscious and hot in the background throughout the following scene

Here, where the reeds are soft and wet. *whispers* Like me.

It will be time for you to cum soon. But you will do it inside me. Our heat will burn as one fire, our spirits merged in an instant of passion and joy, and then, your body will never even remember it was hurt. I've healed so many in the heat of love. I am good at this. I will make you feel so … so … good.

I promise.

Sit down, dear human. Right here by the water. I will sit in your lap. I will dance in your lap. While the other elfgirls moan and gasp with their fingers in their soft, tight pussies.

soft little sounds of need Mmm. Human. I sway my hips. Lift my breasts. My nipples hard little points. My face flushed, my hair dripping and wet. I gleam with water and starlight. Head back. Hands on your powerful human chest. Feel me dance, lithe and supple as when I dance for my goddess in the temple. Feel me, mortal. Naked and wet and yours.

softly For one magnificent night, I am all yours.

Look at me. My deep elven eyes, the sweet curve of my ears.

My lips welcoming and sweet. This body I've devoted to my goddess is feminine ... elven ... *whispers* sacred.

moans You're so hard against my mound. How my sisters tormented you, sweet boy. *sultry* You're staring at my tits. Your hands are tied up. You can't touch. Mmm. You must be on fire from the slick heat of me. The scent of me. The scent of six elfgirls in heat. Needing to be fucked.

I'll lean closer. Here ... here are my tits. Yes, kiss them, mmm, yes, good boy. Oh, kiss my holy tits! Kiss my sacred elven tits! Ah! lick my nipple! Yes! Yes! Ah! You bit me! We really HAVE helped you recover from that goblin camp!

squeals Oh, mortal boy, be gentle with my tits! Be gentle! *moans*

Oh, let me kiss your mouth.

kissing, moaning into his mouth

I like how you kiss.

kissing, moaning

There, I'll rub myself on your cock right there, right there. You are SO hard. Oh mortal, mortal, I'm going to put you inside me now. Lick my breasts, and I'll slide this hard human cock inside me! Ah!

she squeals in pleasure as he enters her

gasping for breath Oh human! It's ... been so long since I had a ... a human in me ... I nearly forgot ...

she cries out wildly

moaning and grunting as he thrusts

trying to remember how to breathe Oh yes, fill me. How you stretch me!

panting

Oh my goddess, I'm so full.

wet sounds

Mmmn! Yes, yes.

moaning

Oh, human. You get to fuck me tonight. You get to cum in me. You get to cum in my pussy. My tight elven pussy. Oh, you're so fucking good in me! Oh goddess! I'm going to grip … and squeeze … and fuck your cock. While my sister elves scream with me under the stars.

We're going to scream for you.

We're going to scream for you!

Make us scream!

moaning as her orgasm gets closer

Oh yes, yes, yes, I'll ride that cock. I'll RIDE that cock! Unnh! Unnh! Unnh! Suck my nipple, mortal, ohhhhhhh yes, mmm, your mouth! Your cock! My goddess has given us ot each other tonight!

wet sounds intensify

wild with heat Feel me swivel my hips, slide up and down your cock! Your hard beautiful cock! This is what I want! This cock! This cock! This is everything I want tonight! My tits bounce against your chest! Oh mortal, fuck me! Fuck me! Fuck me, fuck me!

Oh my pussy is FIRE! Kiss me, wild human boy, kiss me! Kiss your luscious elfgirl!

kissing, passionate and hot

for a few moments, she is grunting, muffled, into his mouth, as she rides him

Yes yes YES YES

Do you hear my sisters' moans? Do you? Do you? Oh, make us cum, mortal! Make us cum! Make us cum, make us CUM!

moaning as they all hurtle toward orgasm

SASHA. Cum!

ELENA. Cum!

VANNA. Cum for us!

ALTARA. Give us your cum, you sweet boy!

ALL. Cum, cum, please please CUM, beautiful human! Cum! You're making us cum! You're making us cum!

KAI. Cum, mortal! I command it! Cum inside her! Let go and CUM! CUM!

they all orgasm, so beautiful and passionate under the stars

they make breathless sweet noises for a few moments, after

KAI. *she lets out two triumphant victory whoops* That felt GOOD! This is the BEST way to end a day of sweat and battle!

ELENA. *moans* I am dead. Slain with pleasure! This cute little elf-thief is slain! *giggles*

VANNA. The whole forest knows you made six elfgirls scream in orgasm, you human pleasure-god.

SASHA. Mortal man, we burned for you under the stars tonight. Now we're soaked and shaking.

ALTARA. *panting* I can't even breathe.

CELDEA. Oh … wow. My insides are sticky and hot with your cum. So much cum. *sultry* I really like it. Mmmn, I'm going to hold your cock inside me a while. Keep all your cum in me. Here, in the soft night by the starlit pool. Lay back. Let me lie here on top of you, kissing your neck.

kissing

Mmmn. The line of your jaw.

kissing

Your mouth. Mmmn.

kissing

Your cheeks.

kissing

Your eyelids. One.

kissing tenderly

Then the other.

kissing

Join me, sisters. He needs our kisses after sex. Our warm, bodies pressed softly to his. Come join me.

splashing sounds as they do

Press yourself to the human we rescued. Let's keep him warm and safe tonight. Press your tits to him, your thighs. With all of us to keep him warm …

VANNA. Is he healed?

ALTARA. Oh, he is SO healed.

ELENA. Just look at his flushed face.

SASHA. He's soaked in sweat, mmmm.

rustling as they lay down beside him

ALL. Mmmn, human boy, sweet boy, mmmn, we'll keep you safe tonight, just sleep with us warm beside you … mmmn, oh human, good boy, good boy, good boy …

lots of kisses and soft, sweet sighs and afterglow sounds

CELDEA. You're going to sleep tonight in a heap of warm, sexy elfgirls.

VANNA. A luscious paladin …

ELENA. A hot-as-fuck little thief and rogue …

SASHA. A fiery sorceress!

ALTARA. A ranger with a soaked pussy.

CELDEA. A cleric with tits soft as the dawn and a cunt that clenches so tight.

KAI. A devious greenwitch, a druid who will dominate you and inflame your wildest instincts.

They keep making soft little sounds as they snuggle in

CELDEA. I'll keep your cock so warm in me. *whispers in his ear* Just stay in my pussy, stay in my wet pussy. This wet elven pussy is for your cock tonight. We rescued you. We saved you.

KAI. We fucked you. *whispers in his other ear* Tied-up human boy. I know JUST what I'm going to do with you once my sisters fall asleep.

CELDEA. *whispers* Sweet, lovely boy.

KAI. *whispers* You are … MINE. My good boy.

sensual kissing sounds

soft whispers of "beautiful boy"

soft kisses

the scene ends

RAVISH A GIRL

Made in the USA
Columbia, SC
16 November 2024